THE MEDIC

THE WOMEN OF WHITE SANDY

SARAH M. ANDERSON

ISBN-13: 978-1-941097-61-8
Printed in the U.S.A.

Dedication

To Melissa Jolly, who didn't kill me when I woke up before the crack of dawn to start Clarence while we roomed together at a conference. Best roommate ever!

Acknowledgements

I could not have written this book without the generous help of the following people: Kurt Riggs, for making sure my Navy terms were shipshape, Amy Short for reading Clarence first, Melissa Jolly for being continually awesome, and Heidi Moore and Jill Marsal. Deepest thanks go to Mary Dieterich for editing and Leah Hanlin.

Chapter One

Clarence Thunder pulled into the parking lot at the White Sandy Clinic and Child Care Center and shut off his truck. He yawned as he rubbed his eyes. Man, it was early. Not even six in the morning.

But the parking lot was empty. Just like he wanted it to be. He had a pound of some fancy flavored coffee, a Matchbox car, and a plan.

He got out of the truck and opened up the Clinic. So far, so good. He'd been half afraid that Nobody Bodine, the night janitor, might still be lurking around. If Clarence was going to make a fool of himself over a woman, he didn't want an audience for it.

But the place was empty, so he got the coffee going. The whole time, he rehearsed what he was going to say when Tammy Tall Trees showed up.

"Hey, Tammy—I made you some coffee."

But the more he rehearsed it, the weaker it sounded. Hell. He didn't know what else to do, though.

For the last four months—ever since the Child Care Center had opened up right next door to the Clinic, Tammy Tall Trees had been arriving at six thirty every morning, along with her three-year-old son, Mikey. And the first thing she did was make coffee.

Clarence got to work about seven—give or take. He operated on Indian time, which meant that sometimes he got here at seven fifteen, sometimes he got here at eight. Didn't matter much. He was the head nurse at the Clinic. It didn't function without him.

At first, when Tammy had started getting here before him, she'd said, "Clarence, I made the coffee." They'd exchanged pleasantries about the weather or people they knew. That was how Clarence found out that Dr. Mitchell's sister, Melonie—the one who'd come out to run the Child Care Center—had somehow fallen for Nobody. Clarence still couldn't figure that one out, but who was he to judge?

Then, after a moment or two of Clarence and Tammy chatting, either a kid or a patient would show up and Clarence would go to his side of the building while Tammy went to hers and that was that.

But recently, in the last month, Clarence had noticed a change in their little morning ritual. Instead of saying, "I made *the* coffee," Tammy had started saying, "I made *you* coffee."

And maybe that wasn't much. One word. Three little letters. That didn't say much about whether or not she was interested in him, did it?

Except…

Tammy had a way of looking at him now that he was pretty sure she hadn't been doing back when she started. She'd hold her cup of coffee up against her lips and blow on it gently—she was a gentle woman—and then, she'd look up at him through her thick lashes and he'd see the corners of her mouth curve up at the same time a pretty blush would dust her cheeks and *damn* if it didn't hit him like a ton of bricks.

That look combined with those three little letters—that had to mean something, right?

Clarence had never been particularly good with women. He was big, he could be mean when he had to be—all things that could appeal to women with a thing for bad boys—but he was a nurse. When he'd joined the Navy right out of high school and gotten off this rez for a decade, being a male nurse—a Lakota Indian male nurse at that—had *not* been the way to score with the ladies. It had been the shortest path between Clarence and a punch line.

But it was a job—a job he was good at. He didn't have the head to be a doctor, but he was good with people and had a strong stomach. And because he had a regular job with a regular paycheck—hell, ever since Dr. Mitchell had come out and started paying him with real money, it was even a decent paycheck—Clarence had been able to save up a little and get some nicer things. Like his truck. The Dodge Ram was only three years old and it ran real good.

That had to be a point in his favor, he decided as he filled up the coffee pot. Clarence didn't know much about whoever Mikey's father was. Tammy's sister, Tara—who was the receptionist at the Clinic—only referred to him as 'that dickbag,' which was a sentiment salty enough to make Clarence blush, old seaman that he was.

As far as Clarence could tell, Tammy was pretty much on her own. Well, sort of on her own. She lived with her mom, who helped take care of Mikey. Flo Tall Trees was more like Tara—brash and outspoken and not afraid to tell you when she thought you were screwing it up.

Tammy was different, though. She was quiet and shy. She had a way with the kids that she watched over—she was the one to soothe hurt knees and hurt feelings, whereas Melonie Mitchell was the loud, bouncy, fun one.

Clarence knew that because he'd taken to popping over to the Center when they had a lull—which wasn't often, but still. He'd stick his head through the door and survey the chaos—or the story time, or the snack, or whatever—and there would be Tammy, right in the middle of it all, handing out hugs and encouragement and always with this beautiful smile on her face. Those kids could be crazy, but he'd never once seen her lose her cool.

"Hey, Tammy—I made you some coffee. And I brought Mikey a toy."

Yeah, that was better. The toy car was a key part of his plan. Namely, he was banking on the car buying him five minutes of uninterrupted time. Ten minutes would be better. That was the best he could hope for. Ten minutes to try and figure out if she was looking at him like she was interested, or if she just *really* liked coffee.

God, he hoped she was interested.

He fumbled with the flavored stuff—vanilla bean, the label said. He was out of practice—Tammy had been making the coffee for months now. But finally, after one or two false starts, he got the water dripping. He checked his watch. Six fifteen. Perfect.

Clarence stashed his lunch and did a hurried version of his morning check. The Clinic was his home away from home and he liked to see that it was in proper working order. Shipshape and Bristol fashion, as his

Navy supervisor was fond of saying. Yeah, the Clinic had seen better days, but it did what it needed to.

Clarence had been here for ten years, through five doctors. None had stayed as long as Dr. Mitchell. Of course, none of them had married the local medicine man, either—but Dr. Mitchell had. And then her sister had come out here and gotten together with Nobody Bodine, which was about the craziest thing he'd ever heard. Nobody Bodine could find love with a woman?

If a convicted felon—and a janitor, for God's sake—could win a lady's heart, why couldn't Clarence?

Clarence didn't like being nervous. But this thing, whatever it was, between him and Tammy was making him *nervous*. She was so quiet and kind—what if she wasn't really sending him signals but was just taking pity on him? Poor old Clarence, the freak male nurse who joined the Navy even though he grew up in a sea of grass.

And if he screwed this up? Then he'd have to deal with Tara. She'd been the receptionist for about four years. She did a good job wrangling the patients, but if she thought that Clarence was screwing around with her little sister, she might cut him to ribbons.

"Good morning, Tammy—I picked up some new coffee I thought you might like. And a toy for Mikey."

No, no—too formal, too stiff. Because what if he was wrong? Aw, hell.

Six nineteen. Six twenty-four. Six twenty-eight. The seconds crawled by. Then it was finally six thirty—and she didn't show up. The coffee finished perking and everything but no Tammy, no Mikey.

Panic rolled deep in Clarence's stomach. He shouldn't have tried the fancy stuff—then everyone would know that he'd done something different, that he'd been trying to impress a woman. Tara might cut him to ribbons anyway.

He was about thirty seconds from dumping the whole pot down the drain when headlights flashed through the windows. He sagged in relief as he watched Tammy get out of her rusty old Accord and then walk around to the other side to unbuckle Mikey. She lifted the boy out and hugged him to her chest, where he sleepily rested his head on her shoulder.

Clarence felt himself breathe at the sight. There was something so damn sweet about the woman that called to him. She was a lot shorter than he was and had very generous curves—the kind of curves that he'd heard other women make fun of, back when he was shipping out of San Diego.

But she wasn't fat, not to him. She was…

Tammy was perfect, really. Warm and soft and just right for a man like him to hold.

Mikey kicked out of Tammy's grip and went streaking toward the Center door.

Now was the time to make his move. His small, cautious move. He filled up two mugs and checked to make sure the car was in his pocket. He managed to get the door open without spilling the coffee down the front of his scrubs. "Morning, Tammy. I…" his throat almost froze up. He was forced to 'harumph,' which caused Tammy to pause and turn her full attention him.

Her eyes lit when she looked at him. They just lit up. "Hiya, Clarence," she said in that soft way of hers.

"Mama," Mikey screeched. "I need paper!"

And the light in her eyes—well, it didn't fade but it redirected to her son. "Hang on, hon." Tammy glanced back at Clarence. "One moment—I just need to get him set up."

"No problem," Clarence said. Then he remembered the car. "Hey, Mikey—I got you something."

"You did?" Tammy asked, turning those big brown eyes back to him.

"Presents?" Mikey yelled as he came barreling up to Clarence. "Gimme gimme *gimme!*"

"Now, Mikey," Tammy said in as scolding a voice as Clarence had ever heard her use. "Use your manners. Pleases and Thank Yous."

"Pease Tank You for the present!" The little boy stuck out his hand and waited.

Clarence realized he was still holding both coffees. He handed one to Tammy and fished the little car out of his pocket. "Here you go, kiddo. Have fun."

"A car? YAH!" Mikey grabbed the car and took off.

"Mikey, honey—say thank you!" Tammy called out after him, but the boy wasn't paying attention.

Which was just the way Clarence wanted it.

"Sorry about that," she said, turning those big brown eyes back to him. "He doesn't get new presents very often. He's very appreciative."

"Don't worry about it," he replied, trying to be cool. He took a sip of his coffee and almost spit it back out. It was too sweet and vanilla-y and barely constituted coffee. He choked and started coughing.

Tammy looked alarmed. "You okay?"

"Fine," he managed to get out. "It's early, that's all."

She dropped her gaze and studied her mug. Oh, hell—had he screwed this up? But then she said, "You *are* a little early today."

Then she looked up at him through her lashes, like she wasn't sure what she would see. There was something in her gaze, something hopeful and cautious and nervous and sweet all at the same time.

If there weren't a kid ten feet away, Clarence knew what he'd do. He'd tilt her chin up far enough that he could kiss her pretty lips, her neck, her... everything.

"*Vrooom!*" This sound was followed by the noise of a car crashing into something.

So Clarence did not kiss her. *Be cool*, he thought. *Be cool.* "Figured, you've been making me coffee long enough. It was time I took care of you."

Her eyes widened in surprise as a beautiful blush danced wildly over her cheeks. Too much? Not enough? Hell, he wished he had more practice.

She looked down at her coffee and took a sip. "Mmm," she said, taking a longer drink. His gut tightened as he watched her lips open.

Okay, good. *Great.* Just the smell of this stuff was making his stomach turn, but if she liked it, he'd brew it every damn day for her.

Finally, when half the cup was gone, she looked up at him. "This is the good stuff," she said.

Clarence grinned. She had a little drop of the coffee on her upper lip. He leaned forward. He couldn't kiss her, not in the middle of the Child Care Center but... "You're worth the good stuff." He cupped her face in the palm of his hand and swiped his thumb over her lip. Her eyes were wide open again, but she didn't pull away, didn't turn her head. She just looked up at him, her lips lightly parted. Was she breathing heavily? Was that a good sign?

"There," he said. His voice had gone all hoarse on him, but he couldn't help it. She was warm and soft against his hand—and that was just her cheek.

What would the rest of her be like? Soft and warm and…

Without thinking, he licked his thumb. Instead of the overwhelming sweetness of the coffee, the taste was tempered with something more salty, more delicate.

Tammy.

She gasped as he tasted the tiny drop of her and coffee together. She *was* panting now, her breath coming in short, tight gasps—which did some things to her chest that he was having a hard time not noticing. But he couldn't look at her heaving bosoms—he couldn't look away from her eyes. All that stuff—the cautious, nervous, hopeful stuff? That was all still there. But it was suddenly buried underneath something else—sheer desire. She tucked her lower lip underneath her teeth and leaned back—not away from him, but so that her breasts were thrust out, as if her body was begging him to touch it. To take it.

Hell, yeah, his gut clenched hard. Harder. Other things clenched, too—which was going to be a problem real fast because medical scrubs were not exactly concealing.

"*Vroom—screech*!" This was followed by a bigger crash and crying.

Tammy visibly shook back to herself. "Oh, Mikey—the bookshelf?"

Clarence forced himself to look away from Tammy to the mess that was sprawled all over the carpet in the middle of the room. The boy had hit a bookshelf and knocked a bunch of books off. Plus, he was crying, although he didn't look hurt. "You okay, kid?"

"I'm sorry," Tammy said in an automatic way. "I need to deal with him and…"

"I can help." That way, they could hang out a little more, although if the boy was in between them, that probably meant no more coffee talk.

"That's sweet of you, but he made the mess, he has to clean it up himself. That's why he's crying." She shook her head. "Come on, honey—pick them up. You're all right."

Yeah, the heat that had about brought him to his knees was gone. Tammy went to crouch next to Mikey. They were done.

For now.

"You want me to refill your mug before I get going in the Clinic?" he asked, picking up her cup.

That happy smile? Totally worth shitty coffee. "Would you? That's so sweet. Thank you, Clarence. Mikey, honey, say thank you for the car again."

"Tanks," the boy sniffed, picking up a book and jamming it back onto the shelf.

Clarence went back over to his side of the building and, after dumping his cup down the sink, refilled her cup. The coffee would probably taste funny for days now, but it was worth it.

He took the full mug back over to her. *Now*, he thought. *Now*. "I'll see you tomorrow morning for coffee, right?"

She looked up at him from the floor, a wide smile on her face. God, a woman should not look so sweet when she blushed. She just shouldn't. "I'd like that."

"Me, too."

10

When he got back to the Clinic side, he leaned against the counter, his head swimming.

She was a sweet woman. She liked sweet coffee. And he hadn't scared her off, not even when he'd touched her.

That meant only one thing.

He was going to need more toy cars.

Chapter Two

Tammy moved through the day in a haze. Mikey picked up the books, children showed up, there were snacks—it as if she were sleepwalking through a dream.

Had Clarence Thunder been flirting? With *her*?

Men didn't flirt with her anymore. She was fat. She had a kid. She lived with her mother. She had a job now, so that was good, but she was not the hot property she'd been a few years ago.

Five years ago, actually.

She looked at Mikey, who was telling everyone he could corral about his *awesome* new car and how it was the best car *ever* and it was his favorite. Clarence hadn't had to get him a car but...

Mikey's own father, Ezra, didn't bring him presents. He didn't visit. And most guys didn't have a big interest in a loud, crazy three-and-a-half-year-old boy who wasn't theirs.

"Miss Melonee!" Mikey yelled when Melonie Mitchell showed up at eleven. "Look at my *awesome* car! It's all mine—I don't have to share it or anything!"

"Mikey, I'm going to make you put it away if you can't play nice," Tammy scolded.

"That is an *awesome* car," Melonie agreed as she surveyed the room. "How's the morning been?"

"Good. Really good." Although Tammy wasn't sure if that was because the kids had been on their best behavior or just because she felt like she was floating. There'd been that moment when Clarence had touched her. And not because he'd made a mess or needed a boo-boo kissed or any of that. He'd touched her because...

She didn't know why. Maybe it was because she was messy and he couldn't stand to see coffee on her lips. He was a nurse, after all. He was used to things being neat and clean and sterile.

Whatever the reason, he'd touched her lips in a gentle way and it'd done things to her. Things she wasn't sure she remembered feeling. Things that had been hot and tingling and tight—so tight it'd hurt in the best way possible.

"Yeah?" Melonie looked at her and suddenly Tammy was embarrassed. "How good?"

Okay, so Clarence was a nice guy. A *really* nice guy. He had a good job. And he was good looking—he was like a tank. Plus, he wasn't scared off by Mikey.

But he was at least ten years older than she was. And nice guys like Clarence were hard to come by. No doubt, he could have his pick of women on this rez— or off of it, even.

He couldn't really be interested in her, could he?

"It's nothing," she said to Melonie and headed back to the kitchen to get started on lunch.

Tammy cooked the lunches every day. She and Melonie would feed the kids and get the littler ones bedded down for their afternoon nap, and then Tammy would head home. She worked the morning shift, Melonie the evening shift. It wasn't a full-time job, but the Mitchell Trust, or Foundation, or whatever rich white people named bank accounts when they decided to give money away, was paying her three bucks more than minimum wage to watch kids. She didn't even have to pay to bring Mikey along with her.

Which meant that, after four months, Tammy was beginning to pay off some bills and have money left over. Not much—not enough to buy fancy coffee—but last week she was able to put fifteen dollars into a sock under her bed to save up for Mikey's fourth birthday and she still had twenty dollars left over.

She had a job she was good at, a boss who liked her and—for the first time in her adult life—a feeling of stability. It was a *great* thing.

Melonie let her go, which was nice. Tammy liked working with Melonie but sometimes, Melonie's enthusiasm was a bit *much*. They were friends, but not the kind of friend Tammy could tell about Clarence wiping the coffee off her lip and then licking it off his thumb.

Hell, she didn't even want to tell her sister that. Once Tara got going, it was all over.

Instead, Tammy cooked. She enjoyed the break of cooking lunch. It was one of the few times when she was not watching Mikey. As she boiled the hot dogs and steamed the peas, Tammy thought over the morning again. What had Clarence said?

"It's time I took care of you."

Yes, that was it. That confused her. Had she been taking care of him? Well, she made the coffee. But that was because she got here so early. Sometimes, a parent had a job off the rez and they had to leave early in the morning. So she got to the Clinic by 6:30 for the early drop-offs. It only made sense that she got the coffee going. As a bonus, her super-early mornings with Mikey meant that the boy went to bed about seven, leaving Tammy with some quiet time in the evening.

Plus, Tara was the receptionist at the Clinic and Tammy knew that without her morning coffee, Tara could be a real bitch. So it was a matter of self-preservation, really.

But Clarence usually got in before Tara did.

She'd gotten used to seeing him first thing in the morning. He was a tall man, the kind that was so big most people did a double-take when he walked into a room. He had a good foot on her, at least, and probably outweighed her by a hundred pounds or more. She'd seen him lift people twice her size out of cars because they couldn't walk and he hadn't even broken a sweat.

He was attractive. Maybe not movie-star hot—but then again, she was no starlet herself. Clarence was strong and dependable and kind to the patients. He was kind to kids.

He was kind to her. And that? *That* was attractive.

And the way he'd touched her this morning?

That blew past 'attractive' and went right over into 'hot.'

She thought about Ezra. Once, he'd made her feel hot, too. Of course, Tammy had been a different woman then. Prettier, shyer, more innocent. More willing to believe what a man said and not what he did.

Once, she'd been in love.

15

It hadn't lasted.

That wasn't what this was, was it? This wasn't love. This wasn't even an infatuation. Okay, after the way he touched her this morning? Maybe it was.

Did that make it a bad thing?

She wasn't the same shy girl she'd once been. She knew better now. Actions spoke louder than words, after all.

The hot dogs boiled over. "Oh!" she exclaimed as she shut the heat off. This was not good. It'd been bad enough this morning when she hadn't been watching and Mikey had taken out the bookshelf. But now?

Clarence was distracting her.

She focused on her task at hand. Lunch could be crazy and they had a nearly full house today. If she got lost in rehashing what Clarence had said—*how* he'd said it—*she was worth the good stuff*?

Somehow, she made it through lunch without total disaster. Then Melonie had the kids get the cots out and everyone lay down. Tammy did the dishes while Melonie read them a story.

When she was done, most of the kids were asleep. They'd been doing this long enough that Mikey had trained himself to stay awake. She'd put him down when she got home. Right now, he was laying on his cot, driving his new, awesome car up and down in front of his face.

She loved her son with everything she had. She wouldn't change anything, really. But there were days…

Would Clarence be here super early again tomorrow? The coffee had already been made by the time she'd gotten here, which meant he must have gotten to the Clinic around six or so. That was at least an hour before his normal time. That couldn't have been an accident.

Tara popped her head in, which left Tammy feeling disappointed. Sometimes, Clarence stuck his head in. He'd look around, catch her eye and give her a quick smile. Tara, on the other hand, wanted to talk.

Tammy left Mikey on his cot. She thought she and Tara might be able to talk alone in the kitchen area, but Melonie followed them back. Wonderful. To hide her nervousness, Tammy picked up the rag and wiped the counter down again. "Yeah?"

"What the *hell* kind of coffee did you make this morning?" Tara huffed in disgust. "It tasted like a vanilla jelly bean died in there or something."

Embarrassment flooded Tammy's cheeks. Was there any way to do this that didn't involve mentioning Clarence? "Um… actually, I didn't make the coffee today."

Tara gaped at her. She was always being dramatic like this. "If you didn't, who did? Don't tell me that freak—" she bit the words off as she looked at Melonie.

They all knew who Tara considered to be the freak—Nobody. Melonie gave Tara one of the meanest looks Tammy had ever seen on her. It looked more like Dr. Mitchell's sneer than Melonie's normally good-natured smile.

"Clarence made it," Tammy blurted out before Melonie could respond or Tara could make things worse. "He thought… he thought everyone might like a change."

Which was not true. But it also beat the hell out of what had really happened.

Tammy was pretty sure he'd gotten it for her and her alone. And if he had, she wanted to keep that secret close to her heart for just a little bit longer.

Her admission was enough to break the tension. Tara huffed and said, "Since when does Clarence try new things?"

"Maybe you should keep an open mind," Melonie snipped. "Or consider the possibility that you're not always right about something."

Whoa, this was going downhill fast. "Right, well, I've got to get Mikey home," Tammy said into the bristling silence. Tara might like to throw down and Melonie might be happy to defend her man, but Tammy wanted nothing to do with a catfight. She dumped the washcloth into the sink and pushed between the two women and out into the main room.

Mikey's eyes were half closed. He'd fall asleep in the car and she'd lay him down in his own bed for two hours of quiet. And today, she needed that quiet.

"Come on, sweetie," she murmured as she picked him up.

"Car, Mommy. Car." He stuck his thumb in his mouth.

"Of course." She crouched down so she could grab the car. She turned to wave to the other women and silently prayed that they wouldn't kill each other—or, if they did, they wouldn't wake the children.

She wanted to warn Clarence that she'd outed him as the producer of the weird coffee. And she really wanted to tell him that it was *good* coffee, no matter what Tara might say. But, assuming Tara wasn't in a fistfight with Melonie, both women would notice that she'd gone to talk to him. And that made her nervous. Maybe Melonie wouldn't say anything, or she'd keep it short because little pitchers have big ears or whatever.

But Tara? She'd get home from work about dinnertime. And if *she* thought there was something going on between Tammy and Clarence, Tammy might never know peace again.

So Tammy did not warn Clarence. She did not tell him she liked the coffee. She didn't even thank him again, which made her feel ungrateful. She just loaded her sleepy boy up into his car seat and drove home.

When Tara got home from work, Tammy did not ask if her sister had given Clarence a hard time about the fancy coffee. And she did *not* ask if Clarence had said whether or not he'd make the fancy coffee again.

But she wanted to. She really wanted to.

When she went to bed that night, she set her alarm ahead fifteen minutes.

Just in case.

Chapter Three

Getting up early one day was hard. Getting up early two days in a row?

It sucked. Big time.

Clarence couldn't stop yawning as he made the coffee. He was pretty sure he wasn't making it the same way he'd made it yesterday, but he couldn't remember how much he'd put in. So he just guessed. Either it'd be close and Tammy would like it or it'd be weak and maybe Tara wouldn't whine about how all the coffee tasted funny.

He rubbed the back of his neck as the coffee dripped. Tara had been all over him after lunch, complaining about how the coffee tasted weird and no one asked him to buy some crappy flavored stuff. She'd been slamming drawers and snapping at patients, too—Clarence wasn't sure if that was all the coffee's fault or if there was something else going on.

Man, he was beat. He'd driven all the way to Rapid City last night and bought some more toy cars. He'd also grabbed some crayons and coloring books and he'd found some toy trains that looked cool, so he got a couple of those, too. Hell, he'd even thrown in a bouncy ball for good measure. Anything small and cheap that might buy him a few uninterrupted minutes with Tammy.

That was, if she wanted a few uninterrupted minutes with him. Yesterday morning, he'd have felt pretty good about that. But after Tara got done ragging on him?

Tara and Tammy lived together. Tara might not think Clarence was good enough for her sister. She might talk Tammy out of… whatever this was. Accepting his coffee and his gifts for her son.

He did not want to go through Tara to get to Tammy. He'd worked with Tara long enough to know that wouldn't go his way.

As he stood there, contemplating his next move— he had a toy truck in his pocket today—he heard a car door shut. He panicked as he looked at the clock—six fifteen? She was early—the coffee wasn't ready yet!

For lack of a better plan, Clarence went to meet Tammy. He got there just as Tammy lifted a very sleepy looking Mikey out of his seat. "Morning," he said in a quiet voice. "Let me get the door for you."

Tammy looked up at him with that shy smile he liked on her so much. "Hiya, Clarence," she said as she slipped past him into the Child Care Center.

As she went past, Mikey said, "Car?" Or at least, Clarence thought he said car. It was hard to understand, what with his thumb in his mouth.

"Sorry," Tammy said as she made her way over to the couch along one wall of the Center. "He was just so proud of his new car yesterday. Mikey, honey, don't demand presents, okay?"

Mikey responded by shaking his head no and burying his face against Tammy's neck.

Clarence felt pretty good about that, actually. The car had worked. Good thing he had another one. "I brought him another one."

Tammy paused and then turned to look at him, one eyebrow raised. Mikey just stuck out his hand. The poor kid was obviously just as tired as Clarence was.

"Mikey," she said, still giving Clarence that questioning look, "if Mr. Clarence gives you another toy car, will you lay down on the couch and play quietly?"

The little boy nodded, thumb still in his mouth.

So Clarence forked over the toy and watched as Tammy gently laid him out on the couch. "He seems tired today," Clarence said.

"We got up early." As she said it, Tammy's cheeks started to color up. She patted Mikey's back as he slowly rolled the new toy back and forth in front of his eyes. It was a tender thing to see. Clarence didn't know much about the boy's father—beyond he was a dickbag, that was—but Tammy sure seemed to love her son.

He waited until she'd stood. "Why?"

"Why what?" She didn't meet his gaze.

"Why'd you get up early today?" He shouldn't ask. He shouldn't push her into a corner like this. But dang it, he wanted to know. Maybe someone was dropping a kid off early. Maybe she really liked weird coffee. Or maybe... maybe she was here for him.

"I could ask the same thing of you," she demanded. She stuck her hands on her hips and tried to look fierce, like her sister did. It did not come naturally to her. "This is two days in a row you've been over an hour early."

Now. *Now.* The boy was quiet and no one else was around. Clarence could do this. He *had* to. He would be kicking himself from now to kingdom come if he didn't. "I wanted to see you."

The effort of saying those words—in a voice that was somewhere between casual and serious without sounding stupid or anything—made him want to slump back and suck in air.

Especially when he saw her reaction. Her eyes went wide and huge again as her mouth fell open. He'd like to close it for her, but he didn't even have the pretext of coffee today.

Coffee! That's what he was missing this morning. "I'll, um, I'll be right back. Coffee's probably ready by now."

He turned to go—and heard her footsteps behind him. "Clarence?" she said when he reached the door that separated the Clinic from the Center. "Clarence, wait."

What could he do? He wasn't a coward who'd walk away from a woman just because he couldn't figure out the best way to hit on her. So, halfway through the door, he paused and turned. "It's, um, it's the kind you like. The good stuff," he told her. God, to be smooth.

"The kind everyone else hated?" She stepped toward him, closing the distance. A small smile quirked up at her lips

Tara. Damn it.

"Did they give you a hard time?" She'd reached the doorway now. She lifted her hand and, after a moment's hesitation, placed it on top of his hand, the one holding the door open.

"Dr. Mitchell didn't care much for it," he admitted.

Actually, what she'd said had been, "Who the hell ruined the coffee pot?"

23

But right now, Clarence didn't care much about how he was going to get dressed down by both Tara and Dr. Mitchell because Tammy's hand was on his— warm and soft and pulsing with desire. Or maybe that was just his pulse racing because *she* was touching *him*. There was no misreading this signal, no trying to guess what she was really thinking.

Tammy looked back over her shoulder and Clarence followed her gaze. Mikey was still laying on the couch, one thumb in his mouth as he rolled the truck forward and back.

Then she turned back to him, her eyes lit with a new fire. She lifted her hand but instead of pulling away from him, she slid it up his arm until she had placed her palm flat against his chest, right over his heart. "But you made it for me again anyway?"

"Yeah," he said, his voice hoarse as blood pounded in his ears. He covered her small hand with his big, rough one.

She dropped her gaze, but then looked up at him through her lashes. Clarence leaned down so he could hear her better. "Why?"

"Because," he said. He needed another arm. He didn't want to hold this door open any longer. He wanted to pull her into his arms and let the door swing shut behind them and for one glorious minute of privacy, he wanted to kiss her like she'd never been kissed before.

Her breath was coming faster now—panting again, like she'd been yesterday when he'd touched her first. When he'd tasted just a drop of her.

"Because why?" Her fingers dug into his shirt, pulling him down to her level so slowly that it hurt.

"Because I care more about what you think that what they think."

Her whole face—well, it didn't light up, not like he'd shoved a flashlight under her chin or anything, but she just got this radiant look about her that made it obvious that he'd said the right thing.

God, she was pretty. He was glad he'd made her look like that, but it wasn't enough. He wanted to lay her out in a bed and make a whole lot more than just her face radiate with joy.

Then she pushed him. Not hard—not like she wanted him out of her way or anything. Hell, she didn't even let go of him.

She just pushed him through the doorway. He was forced to let go of the door, which swung shut behind them. The door was glass, which didn't exactly provide a lot of privacy, but she adjusted her grip on his shirt and directed him to the right.

He knew he was grinning like an idiot, but he couldn't help it. There was nothing subtle or sweet about this. She wanted him. He wanted her. And damn, that was *something*.

She didn't spin him around and pin him against the wall, although he would have let her do just that. Instead, she sort of side-stepped so that her own back was against the wall of the Clinic. And once the door was shut—dividing the sounds of the two clinics, if not the sights—she stopped pushing and pulled him down to her.

"I wanted to thank you yesterday," she breathed as she looped her other arm around his neck and drew him into her.

"Thank me today," he managed to say.

There were no more words. His mouth met hers tenderly at first but then?

She opened her mouth and sighed into him. Her breath—sweet and clean—filled his nose until she was all he could taste, all he could smell—and all he wanted to touch. He didn't even want to close his eyes and miss the way she looked when he kissed her.

He let go of the hand that was still holding onto his shirt and finally did what he'd been wanting to do—he wrapped his arms around her waist and lifted her to his lips. Suddenly one kiss wasn't enough. How long had it been since he'd kissed a woman? Since a woman had kissed him back like this? A long damn time, that was for sure. He needed more.

He touched his tongue to her lips and she made a little sound in the back of her throat, something high and tight and hungry sounding. He couldn't help himself. He leaned into her, pressing her against the wall so he could feel her breasts against his chest—feel the warmth of her body pushing his temperature up higher and higher.

He started to run his hands down her back so that he could grab at her bottom and feel how it filled his hands when she pushed. Her chest was heaving—hell, he was pretty sure he was breathing hard, too.

"I need to get back," she whispered into the quiet of the Clinic.

"Yeah," he managed to say. He knew that—Mikey would wake up some more or someone would show up with a kid or, God forbid, Tara would get here and catch Clarence and Tammy in this position. But he didn't let go of her, not yet. He held her to his chest and tried to get his pulse to go back to normal.

He didn't know how he was going to do that. He didn't feel normal, not anymore.

"Maybe," she said, her voice muffled against his chest, "I'll get here a few minutes early tomorrow. For the coffee."

"Yeah. It's great coffee," he lied. He swallowed, trying to sound less like a love-struck teenager and more like a grown man, for crying out loud. "I can bring you coffee. While you're watching Mikey." He swallowed again.

"Right. Mikey." When she pushed this time, he took a step back. "I need to keep an eye on him. When he wakes up…"

"Yeah," Clarence nodded, like he knew what she meant. "You go. I'll be over in a moment. With the coffee."

She giggled. Then they heard Mikey call, "Mommy? Mommy!"

"Oops." Tammy hurried back into the Center, leaving Clarence alone with his hormones.

It didn't seem right that a woman as sweet and soft as Tammy could give him such a raging hard-on, but the proof was not only unavoidable, it was making walking damn inconvenient at the moment.

Somehow, Clarence got back to the coffeemaker, which had finished. He poured her a big mug and then forced himself to swig some down. The sweetness was pretty much how he remembered it. "Ugh," he said, trying to get the taste off his tongue. But it worked. It was hard to think about sex when his taste buds were trying to commit suicide.

He poured a second mug for Tammy and then dumped the rest of the coffee down the sink. He filled the carafe with water and ran it plain. Maybe that would flush the flavor out of the thing. If not, he was going to have to come up with a plan. Coffee makers were, what? Twenty, thirty bucks? He could buy a new one to make Dr. Mitchell and Tara less bitchy. Might be worth it.

He carried both the mugs over. No one else had shown up. Mikey was now back on the floor, making more 'Vroom!' noises as he raced the new truck around in circles. Tammy was sitting in the middle of the couch, looking like she couldn't believe what had just happened.

Clarence hesitated, then made a decision. He stepped over Mikey and sat down on the couch next to her. "Here," he said, handing her the first mug.

"Thank you," she murmured, leaning toward him ever so slightly. Her shoulder touched his.

"Welcome."

"Mikey," she said, sounding more like her normal self, "what do you need to say to Mr. Clarence?"

"Pease Tank You," Mikey said without looking up.

Clarence laughed. "Yeah, he's got the basics down." Then he pitched his voice down to a whisper. "I got some more cars and stuff at home, if that'll help keep him happy while we discuss… coffee."

A fire-red blush raced over Tammy's cheeks as she studied her mug. *Damn*, Clarence thought. Too much. He'd scared her off.

"You're going to spoil him," she said in a too-quiet voice.

"Oh. Okay. No problem." How had he screwed this up? He couldn't even tell which part he'd screwed up. Did she not like the implication that they wouldn't discuss coffee at all or him getting toys for the kid? Or, worse—both?

They sat there for a moment in tense silence, watching the boy play. Mikey was definitely waking up. Each 'Vroom' was getting louder and the path of the car getting wilder. Clarence could see how it wouldn't be much longer before he was knocking shelves over again.

Outside, a car door shut. "I better go." If it was a parent with a kid, Tammy would need to focus. And if it was Tara, Clarence needed to get the hell away from Tammy. "You want me to leave you this second cup?"

That got her to look up. "Do you mind?"

"Nope. I got it for you. I'm just glad you like it."

She dropped her gaze again, but he saw this time she was smiling in that small way of hers.

Clarence decided to beat a retreat before he did something else stupid. He got back into the Clinic side just as Tara was walking through the door. "What's up?" she asked, eying him suspiciously.

"Nothing," Clarence defended, probably too quickly.

"Really," Tara said, clearly not buying it. "Did you make more of that God-awful coffee?"

"I'm cleaning out the pot," he said, heading back to do just that.

"What the hell, Clarence? Why are you destroying the coffee maker? You can't like that crap."

"I'll fix it," he called back. Eventually. He really didn't want to drive back to Rapid City tonight, too. He wanted to do his time and then go to sleep for as long as possible.

Tara muttered something that sounded like a

curse behind him, but he ignored her. After almost five years of working together, he was good at it.

He knew a lot about Tara. She had a girl named Nelly with Rebel's brother Jesse, although they didn't live together now. Tara had finished some secretarial classes and knew how to file. She ran the business side of the clinic well, so Clarence couldn't complain too much. Before Tara had taken over, he'd been trying to do the paperwork and the nursing, and he wasn't any good at paperwork.

But what did he know about Tammy? She was younger than Tara by a couple of years. She lived with her mom. She had Mikey, who was three or four. Mikey's father was a dickbag and basically out of the picture.

But beyond that, he actually didn't know much about her. She got along okay with Tara. At the very least, Tara didn't spend much time complaining about Tammy. She saved that for Jesse.

How old was Tammy? Had she gone to college? She couldn't be more than twenty-five. Could she really be interested in an old man like Clarence? He was pushing forty and most days, forty felt a hell of a lot like it was pushing back.

The coffee pot was done running the water. Clarence dumped it and made coffee with the regular stuff. He hoped it didn't taste too funny. He really needed the caffeine at this point.

Once it was going again, he turned back to his work. And about jumped out of his scrubs when he found himself face to face with Tara. "What?" he demanded defensively.

"What's going on?" she demanded.

"What do you mean, what's going on? I'm making coffee."

"And you're doing a damn lousy job of it." Tara looked him up and down, as if she could see evidence of the kiss on his scrubs. "Is there something going on between you and Tammy?"

Clarence panicked, which was ridiculous. He'd sewn guys back together who'd accidentally discharged their weapons or walked into a rotor blade back when he'd been in the Navy. He should not be scared of a receptionist with an attitude problem.

But he was. Tara was the biggest obstacle he had to get around to get to Tammy. He didn't want to say *no* because that wasn't true and if Tara told Tammy what he said, it might make Tammy mad. But he didn't want to say *yes* either, because he did not need to deal with Tara all day long—all week long. It was only Tuesday.

So instead, he said, "Why would you think that?" and tried to shove his way past Tara.

"Because…" Tara followed him as he headed for the supply closet. "You never make me coffee and you never make Dr. Mitchell coffee."

"Bull. I make coffee."

"You *like* Tammy?" Tara said it like she had discovered a grass snake in her shoe. "*Seriously*?"

"I've got work to do." At this point, he would scrub toilets with a toothbrush if it got him out of this conversation.

He unloaded the sterilizer and tried real hard to ignore the pricking at the back of his neck that meant that Tara was glaring at him. He was not having this conversation, not with Tara—not with anyone.

31

Sarah M. Anderson

They stood there like that, him unloading the sterilizer and Tara trying to stare him to death, for a good two or three minutes before she said, "You break my baby sister's heart and you'll have to deal with me."

Like that was a news flash. "First off, I already deal with you five days out of the week, so if you're trying to scare me, you're doing a lousy job of it." Which was only partly true. He knew that, if Tara put her mind to it, she could make his life a living hell. "Second off, I'm not out to break anyone's heart." Especially not Tammy's. But he kept that part to himself. He gathered up his clean instruments and said, "Now, if you don't mind, I have a Clinic to run."

He was surprised to see a confused look on Tara's face, like she wasn't sure if she could trust him or not. He shouldered past her and began to get things set up.

She walked past him and, after only a moment's hesitation, sat down at her desk and began to pull files. Which meant she was going to let it drop.

For now.

He didn't know how long of a reprieve he had.

Chapter Four

"Mommy?" Mikey said in his almost-awake voice when he got up from his nap.

"Yes, baby?"

He gave her the look that, in a mere ten years, would morph into a true teenage eyeroll. "I'm not a baby, Mommy."

She swooped him into her arms and kissed him. "You'll always be my baby, baby." He shrieked and giggled as he squirmed in her arms, but he didn't break free. "Now, what's up?"

"Is Mr. Carence gonna keep bringing me toys?"

It wasn't exactly the $10,000 question, but it was maybe the $1,000 follow-up question. Because it sure seemed like Mikey getting presents went along with Tammy getting that sweet coffee—which all seemed to fall away under the $100,000 question—Was Clarence going to kiss her again?

No, that wasn't really the question. The real question was, was Clarence just playing—or was there something more to that kiss, those cups of fancy coffee?

Tammy had been played once. She had no desire to repeat the experience.

But she had a lot of desire, actually. Desire that she worked very hard at ignoring because the last time she'd followed her heart over the edge, she'd wound up pregnant and alone at twenty.

She had absolutely no desire to be pregnant and alone—again—at twenty-four.

"I don't know, baby. But maybe we should write a thank-you letter to Mr. Clarence. It's always good to thank someone. Why don't you find some paper and draw him a picture?"

Mikey hopped down and went to look for his crayons. And, just like she had approximately every thirty seconds all day long, Tammy thought back to the kiss.

The kiss. The one that had probably been far too long and had definitely also been way, *way* too short.

Clarence had kissed her. Yesterday he'd touched her lip and then licked his thumb and today he'd skipped the middle part and just licked her lips. God, just thinking about it sent a rush of heat straight through her.

Rationally, she knew it'd been a stupid thing to do. Kissing a man, even if it was Clarence, in the middle of the Clinic while pointedly not doing her job—watching her own son—in the Center? Yeah, that's how people got fired.

But rationale had very little to do with things right now. It was always good to thank someone when they did something nice for you—and hadn't that been what the kiss was about?

She smiled at that little lie. Because it wasn't, not really. That kiss had been about possibly everything in the world *except* coffee.

It'd been about want and need and lust and maybe—just maybe—something more.

For the first time in years, Tammy had felt wanted and needed. And it'd felt *good*. Most days, it felt like she had everything going against her—she wasn't rich, tall, thin or pretty and who could forget the single-mother part?

But today? Yesterday?

She hadn't felt like any of those things. She'd felt like someone who could still feel love. Who could still *be* loved.

Now what? It was all very well and good for a cup of coffee and a kiss to happen in the Clinic—but the kiss was pushing it. Even though she knew the Mitchell sisters needed her and Clarence to keep each side of the place running, Tammy couldn't imagine that the two women would turn a blind eye to their employees getting it on in a supply closet.

Tammy sighed. She wanted to see where this thing with Clarence was going but… She lived with her mother and her sister—privacy was at a minimum. Her mom had a job pulling the night shift at a convenience store and Tara took her daughter Nelly over to see her father Jesse in the evenings. And of course, paying for a sitter wasn't an option, not on her budget.

"I drew Mr. Carence a picture of my truck!" Mikey announced, which snapped Tammy out of her thoughts.

She needed to get dinner going. "That's great, baby. Can you write your name on it?"

That challenge took Mikey a good ten minutes to figure out—the 'm' was always tricky. As she made the Hamburger Helper, Tammy thought and thought. What was she going to do about Clarence?

Tara got home with Nelly and they all sat down for dinner. Usually, Tara talked about the crazy day at the Clinic—they were all crazy days there—but not tonight. Tara just sat there, staring at Tammy.

Which made Tammy more than nervous. She was sweating by the time Nelly carried in the dishes and started to wash them, which was her job around the house.

"Mikey," Tara said in her sweetest voice and Tammy knew she was screwed. "Why don't you go play?"

Tammy panicked. "I'll go help Nelly," she said as she stood.

"I need to talk to you," Tara replied easily, as if she'd expected this response. Then she added, "Please," for good measure, which was a bad sign. Tara was not the most naturally polite person in the world.

Feeling trapped, Tammy sat. "Yeah?"

Tara waited until Mikey was out of the room. "What's going on with you and Clarence?"

As much as she didn't want to show a sign of weakness, Tammy felt her cheeks grow warm and then hot. "Nothing. He's a nice guy."

Tara wasn't buying it. "Why is he making you terrible coffee if there's nothing going on?"

She felt like she was that girl she used to be, the one who was foolish enough to believe what Ezra said to her and then stupid enough to be heartbroken when he bailed, sitting in this exact same seat and trying not to cry while Tara read her the riot act for being dumb enough to get pregnant and then dumped.

She was tired of feeling foolish and stupid.

That's not how Clarence made her feel.

She was not that same girl, not anymore. She was a grown woman with a child and if she wanted to kiss the male nurse, by God she would. "I don't know. Maybe it's because he's a nice guy?" she snapped, rising from the table. "If it becomes your problem, I'll let you know, okay?"

Tara had the damn nerve to shake her head back and forth, like this was a disappointing answer, right up there with the disappointing answer that Ezra had left. Tammy came this close to reminding Tara that she was not, in fact, Tammy's mother and that, in fact, she had also gotten knocked up by a guy who bailed, so she could just get off her high horse.

Sadly, even when she was pissed, it was hard for Tammy to be that rude. So instead she said, "In the meantime, stay on your side of the street, Tara. And I'll stay on mine." Then she purposefully went into the kitchen and began to dry the dishes.

Oh, yeah—there was something going on with Clarence. And she wouldn't mind something more happening. And wouldn't it be great if the something more happened on a regular basis? But she doubted that Tara would offer to babysit after that little 'discussion' and she wasn't the kind of mother who could just leave her son at home.

What was she going to do?

***

Clarence beat Tammy in the next morning, which gave him time to unbox the new coffee maker. He was not in the best of moods. It was early, yeah. Plus, he was still pissed at Tara—hell, he was pissed at himself and he didn't even know why.

He was not a complicated guy. He got up, went to work, came home, went to bed. Repeat. Simple.

And this—this—this *thing* with Tammy was making things complicated.

What had he expected to happen? That Tara would be so appreciative of Clarence paying attention to her little sister that she'd just get the hell out of the way?

He started Tammy's coffee and cleaned the new coffee pot while hers was brewing. This was not a permanent solution but at least it'd get everyone else to stop bitching about the coffee.

His head was a mess and he didn't like it. This wouldn't be worth the hassle, except he didn't want to let Tara steamroll him.

Except… except for that kiss. To hell with Tara. This was between him and Tammy.

He heard the car doors slamming and went to get the door for her. She had Mikey against her shoulder again.

"Clarence," she said in a tight voice that did nothing to help the place his head was in.

Oh, hell—had Tara gone off on her last night? "Tammy," he replied, feeling uncertain again. "I…"

She stopped and pivoted. He couldn't read her eyes. All that tight tension from the last two days seemed long gone and all that was left was a wariness that was not exactly encouraging. "Yes?"

"I brought a coloring book for Mikey today."

The little boy lifted his head up and popped his thumb out of his mouth. "Coloring?"

Clarence pulled the rolled-up coloring book—some $0.99 cent cheapie featuring smiling animals—out of his back pocket and handed it to the kid. "But you have to do a good job. Stay inside the lines and stuff."

"Peas tank you," Mikey said as he wriggled down from Tammy's arms and went to grab a box of crayons that were little more than nubs off a shelf. Then he sat down and started coloring very carefully.

Okay, so the kid still liked him. But Tammy had her hands on her hips and was giving Clarence a look that was way too familiar. "You're going to spoil him."

"It's just a couple of small things. Didn't cost much."

That was clearly the wrong thing to say because a red-hot blush raced up her cheeks and she darn-near glared at him. "Well, it's more than I can afford to give him and I'm the one who'll have to deal with the fallout when you stop giving him presents for no particular reason."

Clarence blinked at her. He'd never heard her say something so rude before. "What?"

She opened her mouth but then appeared to catch herself. "Look, I appreciate your…*thoughtfulness* but this isn't going to work."

"It's not?"

"No, it's not. I mean…" her voice trailed off as she looked at her son, coloring inside the lines as if his life depended on it. "I can't see how it's going to work," she went on in a much lower voice. Clarence had to move a step closer to her to hear her. "I don't have anything to offer you. I live with my mom and my sister. I have a part-time job and a mountain of debt and a child. I *have* to put him first. Whatever this is, I just *can't*."

She said that last part with so much defeat in her

voice that he forgot about the part where she was telling him to stop making her coffee and to stop giving her kid presents. Instead, he acted on instinct— the instinct to make it better, somehow.

"Mikey," he said as he started pulling Tammy toward the Clinic, "I'm gonna talk to your mom for a second. When we come back, I want to look at your pictures, okay?"

"Okay," Mikey said without looking up. He started coloring even harder.

"What are you doing?" Tammy demanded as Clarence all but dragged her through the dividing door. "Clarence?"

He didn't even try to answer her, not in words. Instead, he kissed her—hard. Not the tentative asking of permission that'd happened yesterday.

Today, he kissed her like a man kissed the woman he wanted. Because he wanted her and he'd be damned if he let her talk herself out of it.

He wrapped his arms around her waist and pushed her up to his mouth. He swept his tongue into her mouth and tasted the salty sweetness of Tammy.

There was a painful moment where she didn't kiss him back and he was sure that she'd already made up her mind and he was just making it worse.

But suddenly her arms were around his neck and she sighed into his mouth and the kiss became something deeper, something more.

He could kiss her all damn day, but they didn't have that much time. He had to make every single second count.

"*Oh*," Tammy said when the kiss ended. Her eyes were closed and her brow was creased, although he couldn't tell if it was in disgust or happiness or what. She looked like she was deep in thought.

"Just because you can't see how this is going to work doesn't mean it won't," he told her. He kissed her forehead, right on the crease. "You have to put the boy first, I get that. But let me put you first, Tammy. Let me at least *try*. Because I like you and I think you have a lot to offer me and I hope I have something to offer you. Something more than coffee," he added.

She sort of sagged in his arms. "You do, Clarence. You do. But I don't want to be played for the fool again. I've had quite enough of that in my life."

He gaped at her. "You think I'd—what, that I'd *use* you?"

She opened her eyes and he saw a world of pain before him. No wonder her sister referred to Mikey's father as 'that dickbag.'

"I wouldn't do that, Tammy. That's not what I'm here for. I want…" He leaned down and put his mouth against her ear. "I want something more than *that*. I want you. All of you."

She gasped and jolted in his arms, pressing every part of her against a few really important parts of him. Inwardly, he groaned in pain. Then she said, "But Mikey…"

"Bring him," Clarence said, even though that wasn't his first choice—especially not if Tammy didn't want him to spoil the boy. "Come have dinner with me on Saturday, you and Mikey."

She opened her mouth like she was maybe going to say no but then paused and nodded her head. "I don't want to bring him. I don't want him to get attached if…"

If this didn't work.

41

Clarence kissed her again, trying his damnedest to push that thought right out of her mind. He'd barely gotten started. He wasn't going to think about the end just yet. "Then just you. Let me take care of you, Tammy. Let me make you dinner."

"I can't," she said and at least she sounded truly sorry about it. "Mom works the night shift and I don't think Tara will watch him. She doesn't like this."

"I'm not going to let Tara dictate *us*," he said with more force than he meant, but it was true. "This isn't about her. This is about you and me. If you can't do dinner, what about lunch?"

"Mom would watch him, as long as I was back before she had to go to work." She took a deep breath. "All right. Lunch." Then she cracked open one eye. "Can you cook?"

"I get by." A five-course meal wasn't going to happen but food that tasted good—plus maybe a bottle of wine? Yeah, he could pull that off. "Eleven-thirty?"

"Okay, eleven-thirty. It's a date."

A date. He hadn't had a date in a hell of a long time. It was almost as if he was twenty again, young and stupid on shore leave for the first time in months.

He opened his mouth to say something—what, he didn't know. Did men thank women for agreeing to a date these days or what?—when Mikey called out, "Mr. Carwence? Wanna see my pictures?"

Tammy raised an eyebrow at him in what looked a hell of a lot like a challenge. "Coming," Clarence called out. Then he gave Tammy a quick kiss before he went to get the coffee.

Saturday seemed like both a long way off—and not nearly enough time to get ready.

Chapter Five

Tammy paused long enough to take a deep breath, because she wasn't sure she was going to continue breathing on a regular schedule.

She was really doing this. Well, *this* was just lunch with a work friend. A work friend she'd kissed a couple of times, but still. It's not like she was running off to Vegas with Clarence or anything. Just having lunch.

Alone. With a man who'd held her in his arms and whispered in her ear that he wanted her. A man who had made her coffee every single day since. A man who treated her son well and told her he wanted to take care of her like it was a point of personal pride.

It'd be so easy to just let Clarence take care of her. It'd be a relief, honestly, after three plus years of trying and trying and *trying* so hard to make things work.

But it wasn't just her. She had to keep Mikey in mind. Clarence was being thoughtful and attentive to both of them, but she didn't want Mikey to get attached if this wasn't going anywhere.

She didn't want to get attached if this wasn't going anywhere. She didn't want to fall for sweet words and empty promises again.

This was *just* lunch.

If she kept repeating it, it was bound to be true, right?

Clarence opened the front door before she got halfway up the walk. "Hiya," he said as he came to greet her.

She couldn't remember a time when she hadn't seen Clarence in scrubs but today he was in a gray t-shirt that fit him well and a pair of blue jeans. His close-cropped hair was neat and he just looked good.

Yeah, this wasn't just lunch and they both knew it.

"Hiya," she tried to say, but it came out as a whisper. She tried to clear her throat, but there was this lump stuck about halfway down that was making talking almost impossible.

"It's good to see you in the daytime," he said as he slipped an arm around her waist and pressed a kiss to her forehead. "I'm glad you came."

She felt self-conscious standing here in broad daylight with Clarence's arm around her. What did it matter if someone saw them? Her mom and her sister already knew—or thought they knew—what was going on. Her mom was actually kind of on board with it, too.

"He's a good one," Mom had said when Tammy had managed to tell her why she wanted Mom to hang out with Mikey. "And good ones are hard to come by."

"I don't know that this will go anywhere," Tammy had replied, feeling her face grow hot. "This is just lunch."

Her mom—a woman who had raised two daughters by herself and was now helping to raise two grandchildren—a woman who had a firm grasp on exactly how hard 'good ones' were to come by—had merely smiled. "Well, you have fun, honey," she'd said. "Don't you worry about me and Mikey. We'll have a good time."

So Tammy tried not to worry. She leaned her head against Clarence's shoulder and said, "I'm glad I came, too."

"Lunch is almost ready," he said, guiding her toward his house. "Hope you like burgers and fries?"

"That's fine." She smiled to herself, a feeling of warm satisfaction. It wasn't that the meal was fancy—but he'd made it for her.

She wasn't sure what kind of place she expected Clarence to live in. After all, she lived in a pre-fab house that dated back to the 1980s. Most everyone she knew either lived in the same kind of house or in a trailer that was even older.

At first glance, Clarence lived in the same house she did. But upon closer inspection, she noticed important differences. For one, he had an actual lawn—neatly mowed and green, which meant he was watering it. His house was a bright blue color and had shutters—bright white and hanging straight—on the windows. Along the foundation were clumps of black-eyed Susans and coneflowers in full yellow and purple bloom.

Tammy searched her memory, but couldn't find any recollection of painting her house. Once, she'd tried to plant some flowers around the steps, but they'd died.

"Your place is pretty," she said, not sure if that was the right thing or not.

"Thanks." She looked up at him—was he blushing? Maybe 'pretty' had been the wrong word.

"It's all those years in the Navy. A place for everything and everything in its place." He opened the door for her.

When was the last time someone had held a door for her? "How long were you in the Navy?" she asked as she walked past him.

"Joined when I was eighteen. They put me through nursing school—there was no way I could have afforded it on my own."

She sighed. "I know. I'm still in debt from college." As she talked, she looked around. The inside was what one might call sparse—he had a blue couch and a matching recliner, but he didn't even have a coffee table. Instead, he had a flat-screen TV on a stand that lined up perfectly with the recliner. She could tell from the way the recliner sagged and the couch didn't that he always sat in the chair. The other thing that was surprising was that the entire wall between the front door and the hallway that lead back to the bedrooms was lined with bookcases—huge bookcases that loomed a solid foot over her head and were neatly lined with all kinds of books. She hadn't seen so many books in one place since she went to the library at school.

She had never actually seen a flat-screen TV in person before, just on the commercials. They had a regular old tube TV that got most of the channels but lines drifted up the screen on three of the channels. When it went, she didn't know if they'd be able to get another one.

Clarence grinned down at her. "Come on." He led her through the dining room, which opened into the kitchen. The walls were a bright white without a scuff or crayon mark in sight and the table was nearly completely empty. At home, she didn't have a flat surface that didn't attract piles of papers or toys or whatever, but the only thing on Clarence's table was salt and pepper shakers.

It wasn't that she didn't try to keep a neat house, but with three adults and two kids living in the same small house, keeping things this clean was nearly impossible. She was doing good most days if Mikey didn't add another permanent stain to the carpeting.

"Are you okay?" Clarence asked as he guided her through the kitchen, which was much cleaner than her own, and out the back door onto a tidy little patio, complete with a bistro table set for two with an honest-to-God rose in a little vase.

Tammy pulled up. Where had he gotten a rose?

"This is lovely," she said looking at the spread of food all arranged on platters on the table. Fries and burgers, with corn on the cob and grilled peppers. "This is…" she almost said 'too nice for me,' but she managed to keep that part in her mouth. "Lovely," she managed to finish.

"What would you like to drink? I have some beer, some wine, and lemonade."

"Lemonade." Hadn't that been part of the problem the first time? She and Ezra would go out and get buzzed and wind up in the backseat of his car, too drunk to make sure that the condom was on right. "If you don't mind."

"Nope." Clarence disappeared back into the house, giving her a moment to study her surroundings. His house backed up to a little culvert that was overgrown with scrub trees and the neighboring houses were set off to the side, so she couldn't see into anyone else's windows. It was almost like there wasn't anyone else in the world, just the two of them.

Clarence came back out with two glasses of lemonade and set them down on the table. Then he pulled his chair around so that he was sitting next to her. "Your mom is staying with Mikey?"

"Yes." She didn't really want to bring her mom into the conversation, though. "Tara made herself scarce, so it really wasn't too much of a problem."

"That's good. He's a good kid," Clarence said as they ate.

This was fine. Normal. Just making small talk, getting to know each other. She was not nervous discussing what was the biggest mistake and also the biggest blessing of her life with Clarence. Not at all. "Thanks. He'll be four in a couple of months." She sighed. "When he was born, my mom told me that the days were long but the years were short and it's the truth. I can't believe that it's been almost four years, but just getting through the day sometimes…" She took a long drink, trying to compose her thoughts so that she sounded like a rational woman, instead of one on the verge of dissolving into grateful tears. "I can't thank you enough for being so nice to him. You're probably his favorite person in the whole world right now. He doesn't usually get toys unless it's his birthday or Christmas."

"I wasn't trying to make things harder on you," Clarence admitted, not looking at her. "I was just trying to keep him occupied for a few minutes."

A few minutes where he could talk to her. *Kiss* her.

They ate in silence. The day was warm without being hot as puffy clouds danced over the blue sky. Little by little, Tammy began to relax. Just lunch. Just two friends. This was not a big deal. It was just Clarence.

Except it wasn't and she knew it. They both did.

"So," she said, not wanting to break the comfortable silence but wanting to anyway, "you joined the Navy when you were eighteen?"

"Yup. Graduated high school, shipped out two weeks later. I wanted off this rez so bad," he said, his voice getting distant. "Funny how I wound up back here."

She knew the feeling—wanting off and yet not quite being able to go. "Why?"

"I missed the place," he said, leaning back in his chair. She did the same, casually resting her hand on her armrest.

It didn't stay there for long. Clarence reached over and rested his hand on top of hers. His hand was so much larger than hers was—well, that wasn't surprising. The man was huge. But what was surprising was the little thrill his touch sent through her body, like a long-forgotten first blush.

"After I got my nursing degree, I spent the better part of ten years on aircraft carriers," he went on, his thumb stroking over her knuckles. "Living packed into tight quarters with all kinds of people, surrounded by water and sky. The sky was the same, but nothing else was. I could have re-upped for another tour, but I wanted to come home." He turned to her and grinned. "I saw the world, but I missed home. Never thought I would, but I did."

She'd never even gotten off the rez, except to go grocery shopping. Seeing Rapid City wasn't really the same thing as seeing the whole world. "And you've been working at the Clinic since then?"

"Yup." He sighed, looking around his place. "This was the house I grew up in. My mom died while I was at sea. I came home, fixed it up, started working at the Clinic. It's not exactly exciting, but it's not bad."

"It's amazing," she said. He gave her a look that said he didn't quite believe her. "I wish… I always wanted to get off the rez and see the world."

"But life happens," he said quietly.

"Yeah, you could say that. Mikey happened, anyway." She looked down to where their hands were joined. "This is probably the first time I've left him to do something for myself."

A weird mix of emotions played through her as she said it. She was thrilled she'd done something for herself—but yet, she still felt guilty that she'd left him for something as selfish as a peaceful meal that didn't involve spills or screaming.

Clarence was watching the sky. Thin clouds scurried over the bright blue sky. "Really? You haven't even gone out since he was born?"

"No." Now she just felt ashamed. Who was she going to go out with? There'd been no interest in her, none at all. And truthfully, she hadn't sought that attention out. Something about being knocked up and dumped made a girl wary. "Not since his father left before he was born." She'd gained so much weight while she was pregnant and hadn't managed to lose any of it afterwards. "Not that many men are interested in a—well, in someone like me."

He appeared to think that over. "Well, most men are idiots."

She grinned as she felt her cheeks heat up. "This has been really nice. Much better than just a few minutes in the morning."

He took a drink. "We could do this again."

The way he said it made it sound like… dating. Something that happened regularly. Something that was dependable. "We could."

Clarence squeezed her hand. "Do you want to?"

Want. A few days ago, he'd whispered in her ear that he wanted her and for an electric second, she wasn't the single mother of a young boy but a woman who was being chased by a good man who could reduce her to a quivering mass of jelly with a few simple words.

She turned her hand over and laced her fingers with his. "Did you mean what you said? That you wanted *me*?" She had to force herself to say that last word because it was still so hard for her to believe that anyone would want her. "Because I don't want to be played again and I won't let Mikey get played with me."

Clarence kissed her palm. "You were played?"

His lips were warm against her palm, which was rapidly heating up other parts of her body. She tried to push the desire down. "I was stupid. I was twenty and I had a decent body and I thought…" She'd thought men could be trusted, that love would conquer all and that everything would work out. She'd thought she was smarter than she'd turned out to be.

"You're beautiful," he murmured—and then he kissed her palm again. "I like your body. I like *you*."

51

She couldn't respond to that because she just didn't know how. All she could do was sit there as want—need—started to course through her veins.

Once, she'd liked sex. A lot. But she hadn't had the time to even think about it for the last four years or so, not when she fell into bed in a state of exhaustion every single night.

"You're twenty-four?" he asked, still holding tight to her hand.

"Yeah." Some days she felt so old, but she knew there were people in this world who were still in college, still trying to get it figured out. She'd heard the phrase—a quarter-life crisis. At least that was one upside of Mikey—she simply did not have the time for existential self-doubt. She had to make it through each day, one stinking day at a time.

"I'm going to be forty next year." He announced this as if it were a death sentence he had no desire to carry out. "If that's too old for you, I'll understand. Fifteen years is a big gap."

She looked at him. His gaze was still fastened on the sky, as if he were afraid to look at her—afraid of what she might say.

"Why me?"

His head snapped down and he stared at her. "What?"

"Why me? I'm a broke single mother. I live with my mom and my sister—and you know what that means." He grimaced at the mention of Tara. "You're good looking, smart, you've got a good job and a nice house. You could have your pick of any woman on this rez." She swallowed. It was the truth, but it didn't make it any easier to say it. "So why me?"

Was it just because she was an easy target? Available? Or was there something else going on?

Please, God, let there be something else, she prayed.

He locked his gaze onto hers. "Because you're beautiful and thoughtful and a good mom and when you look at me, I don't feel like the butt of some cosmic joke about a male nurse."

She gaped at him. "Really?" Because that's not how she saw herself. And that wasn't how she saw him, either. "You're not a joke to me, Clarence. You're an amazing man."

That grin—oh, my. "Did you ever consider," he said in a low voice that sent a thrill right through her, "that maybe I already looked over other women and you're the best woman on this rez?"

No. She could honestly say she hadn't considered that option—hadn't even considered it to be an option. She opened her mouth to respond, but nothing came out.

His mouth curved into a smile that darn-near bordered on wicked as he lifted his hand and cupped her face in his massive palm. "Because you are," he whispered as he leaned forward. "You're the best woman on this rez."

"You can't mean that." It was her last gasp at keeping some sort of distance between them—some sort of grip on herself.

And then the distance was gone. "I can and I do." Then his mouth captured her and she was powerless to do anything but kiss him back.

No one could see them. Mikey wasn't about to barge in on them. Tara was nowhere.

This was just him and her. She could do whatever she wanted. The feeling was intoxicating.

He ran his fingers through her hair and angled her head back so he could kiss her neck. "Tammy…"

She pivoted in her chair to give him better access. She was feeling things—things she'd forgotten how to feel. No, that wasn't true—she remembered desire and want coursing through her body. She'd just pushed it all down and locked it away. She'd refused to acknowledge that she still had needs because she wasn't a young woman with a future anymore—she was a mom who put her son first.

Except for right now.

"I want you to stay," Clarence whispered against her skin as he ran his tongue over her throat. "It's fine if you don't, but I want you to."

That was really why she'd come, wasn't it? To see if Clarence was the kind of man she wanted to be with—the kind of man who wanted to be with her? To see if she could let a little of that desire out of the box she'd stored it in. To see if she could still be a woman worth wanting.

And this time, there would be no confusion, no hiding her desire behind alcohol. Clarence liked her. He wanted her. He was not promising her the sun, the moon and whatever stars he could round up. There was no grand talk about the future. Just the present. Just right now.

"Clarence," she told him, promising herself she would not regret this, not like the last time. "Take me to bed."

Chapter Six

Hands down, those had to be the sweetest five words he'd ever heard. But he had to play it cool because somehow, he didn't think that jumping up and going, "Really? AWESOME!" was the most effective form of foreplay.

Instead—trying to be cool—he stood and pulled her up into his arms. "Do you have…" She blushed. God, she was so pretty.

"Yeah." That'd been an important part of his last trip into town—a box of condoms. He might want kids one day—but not today.

He just wanted Tammy.

He swept her into his arms, which made her squeak. "Clarence!"

"I've got you," he told her as he cradled her against his chest. Then he kissed her again, right in the middle of the patio.

She curled her fingers around his shirt, pulling his chest into hers. Right. He needed a bed before she got him so worked up that he couldn't walk. He had to make sure he did this right. She deserved nothing less.

He managed to get the door open with his foot and then he was heading back toward his bedroom. It wasn't fancy—he didn't have matching curtains and bedspreads or anything—but it had his bed and that was the important thing right now.

He carried her inside and set her down on the edge of the bed. "Tell me what you want," he murmured as he cupped her face in his hands. "Tell me what you like."

She blushed again, as if having sex was one thing but talking about it was an entirely different thing. Then she looked up at him through her lashes, just like she did in the morning and he was lost to her. Completely lost.

"I like the way you kiss me," she replied.

So he kissed her again. He took his time. He didn't have to think about anyone walking in on them. He could love on her all day and all night long, if that's what she wanted.

She scooted back on the bed a bit and he kneeled in between her legs, which had the convenient side effect of putting their heads on almost the same level. He wrapped one arm around her waist and cupped her left breast with the other. She gasped at the touch.

"Do you like that?" He felt her body respond, felt her nipple grow hard under his touch. He circled that point with his thumb.

"Oh," she breathed, like she was trying desperately to hold onto... something.

"Yes or no?" When she didn't immediately answer, he slipped his hand under her shirt and found her hard nipple again. "Yes or no?"

"Yes," she gasped. Her back arched into him and she gripped his shoulders. "Yes."

Blood pounded in his ears. He grabbed the back of her shirt and lifted it over her head, leaving her in just a plain white bra that had a hint of lace on the edge of the cups. "So beautiful, Tammy," he growled as he filled both his hands with her breasts. "So beautiful."

He was fighting hard for his self-control because all he wanted to do was peel off the rest of her clothes and bury himself in her body, but he dug deep and focused on her breasts. He kissed the edge of skin right above that little bit of lace as his thumbs teased her nipples until she was panting and moaning. "Oh, Clarence."

"Yeah, babe—let go. Let me…" he relinquished his hold on her breasts but only so he could try to get the bra off. Thankfully, the clasps gave and suddenly, her breasts—truly, one of the best sets he'd ever seen—were free. He lowered his mouth onto the left one and went back to teasing the nipple of the right one.

"Oh, yes," she moaned. She laced her fingers through his hair and held him to her. "Yes, I like that."

"Mmm," he hummed into her skin as he shifted his attention to the other one. He let his free hand drift down over the front of her jeans and down between her legs. "How about this?" he asked as he rubbed against the seam of her jeans.

She gasped, but she didn't pull away. "Yeah," she said, grabbing at the back of his shirt and pulling it over his head. "I want to touch you, too."

She went for his jeans, but he grabbed her hands and held them away from his dick. If she went in hard, he wouldn't last. "Easy," he growled as he pushed her back onto the bed.

It was then, when he was over her and she was looking at him that he saw the tension—the fear—ease back. "I always wondered," she whispered as she looked at his chest. She pulled one of her hands free and ran it down his chest. "Scrubs don't do you justice."

"I'm not as young as I once was," he told her. Once, he'd been ripped with the kind of body that ladies in ports the world over couldn't resist. But middle age had made him less cut, more cuddly.

She thought about that. "No, probably not. I bet you're better."

Clarence grinned before he kissed her again. She wanted better? He'd show her better. He let his tongue taste her lemonade sweetness before he worked his way back down to those fabulous breasts.

He undid the button on her jeans and began kissing down her stomach. Suddenly, she tensed. "No," she whispered as she covered her stomach.

He froze. "No?"

She tried to roll away from him, like she wanted to hide. "Not that. It's—after I had the baby—"

"I don't mind the stretch marks. They're a part of you."

She shook her head. "Not... not this time."

That was a concession he was willing to make. "Maybe next time?" Because he'd like a next time. Several next times.

She didn't meet his gaze. "Maybe."

He wanted her to let go of her self-consciousness but he didn't want to push the issue right now. So he went back to licking and sucking her nipples. When he scraped his teeth over the hard nub, she bucked against him. That was better.

He forced himself to sit back and dig the condoms out of the drawer on his bedside table. Tammy sat up and this time, when she reached for his jeans, he didn't stop her.

For years, Clarence had touched people. That was

the job. He lifted them onto tables and sewed them back together and performed exams and cleaned wounds. But how long had it been since someone had touched *him*?

Way too long, was all he could think when Tammy slipped her hand into his pants and stroked his dick. "Oh, my," she whispered as she pushed his jeans and briefs down. He sprang free, at full mast. "Oh, Clarence."

Then, before he could stop her, she leaned forward and took him in her mouth.

The overwhelming sensation almost did him in. He couldn't speak, couldn't even move as Tammy licked along his shaft and took the head of his dick into her mouth again.

His eyes drifted shut as she swirled her tongue around his tip. He fisted his hand in her hair. He didn't know if he was holding her to him or pulling her back—both, maybe. All he knew was that he was desperate for more and just as damned desperate to make her stop. He was supposed to be taking care of her—showing how he could be good for her, not the other way around. "Tammy…"

"Mmm?" she hummed around his dick, which made telling her to stop impossible.

"God," he groaned, his hips flexing as she took him again and again. But when she started to stroke more than just his dick with her hands while she licked him, he had to pull her away before he lost it. "Easy," he managed to say again, but his voice came out as a strained whisper.

She looked up at him with worried eyes. "Not good? I thought…"

He brushed her hair away from her face and trailed his fingers down her cheek. He could guess what she thought. That the men she'd been with before had always put themselves first, her second. Blow jobs were just as good as sex to a man who didn't care about his woman.

And that wasn't Clarence. "Listen to me, Tammy Tall Trees." His voice came out as a low growl. "You are not allowed to come after I do. I will always put you first. *Always*."

Her eyes widened in shock and he had to wonder if she'd ever really come—or just settled for whatever bone she'd been thrown after blowjobs.

He was having a lot of trouble thinking straight, what with the sheer desire that had him on the brink. "Your jeans," he heard himself say as if from a long distance away. "Take them off."

Her eyes still wide, she nodded. She stood and shimmied out of her jeans. He tried to honor her wishes and keep his gaze on her breasts—because they were really worth studying—but when she finally got out of her jeans and her panties, he couldn't help but spread her before him.

Even though he was straining to be inside her, he pushed her legs open and touched her. He rubbed his thumb over her, listening as she sucked in little breaths.

Oh, she was warm and ready for him. "So wet," he murmured as he lowered his mouth back to her breasts, stroking against her tight little clit as he sucked her nipples.

She gasped and he thought she might put the brakes on again, but it wasn't long before she was writhing underneath him as he went from rubbing her clit to stroking a finger inside her body. "I want you so bad," he told her, because that was the truth and also because talking helped him hang onto the very last thread of his self-control.

"Yes—oh, Clarence!" she moaned as he slipped two fingers inside of her.

Her nails dug into his shoulders as she said it, but he didn't care. This was how he wanted her—full of need that only he could answer. "Yeah," he whispered against her neck as he worked over her body. "You like that?"

Her hips shifted as her inner muscles gripped his fingers. God, he though. *This* woman. *His*.

"Now," she gasped as he stroked in and out, learning her body's rhythm.

"Now?" Was she about to come or—

"I need more, Clarence." Her hips lifted. "I need you inside me—*now*!"

Yeah, he was ready for *that*. "Yes, Ma'am."

He leaned back, rolled on the condom and fit his dick against her. Then he began to thrust. He tried to go slowly, but the feeling of her body engulfing his and her hands on his back and his name on her lips did something to his brain. The next thing he knew, he was plunging into her again and again, harder and faster, making her cry out, "Yes, oh, God—just like that, oh Clarence, *yes*," until her body tightened around his and she opened her eyes and met his gaze as she came and she was the most beautiful woman he'd ever seen, just like that.

She fell back panting and he buried himself deep inside her, feeling the waves of her climax pull his from his body until he came with a roar that he muffled against her neck.

He lay on top of her for a moment, too stunned to think, to speak—to do anything but just *be* in her arms.

"Stay with me, Tammy," he murmured as he kissed her ear, her neck, her lips. "I want you to stay. Whatever it takes, I'll do it."

She didn't answer.

***

Tammy lay under Clarence's weight, trying to think straight and doing a really lousy job of it.

The sex—God, the sex. She'd always liked it before but the way Clarence filled her?

Breathe. Breathe in, breathe out.

Actually, that was kind of hard. He was heavy. But she didn't want to break their connection, not just yet.

Except—except for the things he'd just said.

And even though she knew that Ezra was long gone and probably never coming back, she'd heard the promises that he'd made all those years ago, about how much he loved her and how he'd do whatever it took to make sure that they were together. Anything, he'd said.

Anything but be a father, apparently.

She didn't want Clarence's promises. She didn't want to think about a future and whether or not he'd actually be a part of it, no matter what he said.

She'd just wanted this moment. And she'd had it, briefly.

"I can't breathe," she told him. It wasn't just due to his weight.

"Sorry." He rolled off her and stood. "Be right back."

She lay there for a moment, trying to sort through her thoughts, all while trying to remember to breathe. And no matter how she tried to think it through, she kept coming back to the same question she'd had earlier in the week.

She didn't see how this was going to work. Which had sucked when she'd said it before. But now? Now that she'd had Clarence—now that he'd had her?

She heard the bathroom door open. Quickly, she stood and gathered her clothing, holding the bundle in front of her stomach.

Why didn't this man have any curtains or shades or something to darken the room? *Something* to hide her body?

Clarence strode into the bedroom in all of his naked glory. Wow. He may be in his late thirties, but damn. He had a hell of a body. Maybe not a full six-pack of abs, but his chest—the chest that had been so recently against hers—was enough to make her start to drool.

She didn't realize she'd uttered any words out loud until he turned a suggestive smile in her direction. "You like?" Then he noticed that she was holding her clothes. "Oh. Yeah—the bathroom—just down the hall."

She swallowed down her nerves. "Okay. Thanks."

She got cleaned up and dressed and then just… stood there for a minute, trying to figure out what to do next. How to respond to his 'Whatever it takes,' comment.

Because it would be so damned easy to say yes and let him do just that. To spending time with him. To letting Mikey spend time with him.

63

And she couldn't. She *couldn't*.

Once, she'd believed it when a man had promised to love her, to take care of her. Once.

It would be easy to love Clarence. It'd be *so* freaking easy to throw her lot in with his, to let him take some of the burden off her shoulders.

She couldn't ask that of him. To be a father to someone else's child? Because what would happen when Mikey was, well, Mikey? When he had a bad day, a bad week—when he was a Tasmanian devil of a boy that ruined every single thing that he touched? Then what?

Ezra hadn't even stuck around to see his own kid. She couldn't imagine how, even if he was a 'good one,' Clarence would want to deal with Mikey day in and day out. Because there were days—dark, long days—when Tammy didn't even want to deal with her own son. She wasn't proud of herself on those days, but there it was. Being a full-time single parent was not all sunshine and rainbows.

She stared at herself in the mirror. All she'd wanted from Clarence was to be in the *now*. Why the hell couldn't she get her mind out of the *future*?

Well. She couldn't hide in this bathroom forever. She forced herself to open up the door and walk out.

She peeked into the bedroom, half expecting to find a still-naked Clarence waiting for her, but the room was empty. She stared at the bed—it didn't even look rumpled. Like they'd never had sex on it.

She padded out into the living room, but it was also empty. So was the dining room and the kitchen. It was only when she opened the back door that she found him, sitting in his chair with one refilled glass of lemonade in his hand and a second one—hers—on the table.

In that moment, as she looked at the fresh glass—complete with ice—set near the rose in the vase, she wavered. It'd be *so* easy to love him. That didn't make it a bad thing, did it? That didn't make her weak or stupid, did it? Not like she'd once been, right?

"Can you stay for a little bit longer?" He took a drink. His voice was level. "It's about 2:45. If you need to get home to Mikey, I understand."

Even though he sounded perfectly normal, she was sure she heard a hint of hurt in his voice. She opened the door and stepped outside. "I need to be home by four so Mom can get to work."

He nodded, but he didn't say anything else. His gaze was focused on the sky.

So she sat in the chair that was still close enough to his that she could feel the heat from his body.

The air was tight with tension that hung in that narrow space between their bodies. She could tell she'd offended him and she wanted to reassure him that it wasn't him—it was her. She didn't. Yes, it was the truth, but she knew how it'd sound if she said it out loud and she didn't want to hurt him.

He leaned forward and set his glass back on the table next to hers and then covered her hand with his. "Which part didn't work?"

"Sorry?"

He picked up her hand and kissed the back of it. "Something didn't work for you. Which part?"

She'd never been asked that before—who would ask? Ezra? No. He'd bought the beer and taken her out on a deserted road and told her what she wanted to hear and, yeah, she'd enjoyed it. She'd enjoyed his attention, his promises. But the first time had hurt so badly and she'd made herself not cry because she didn't want to upset him. He'd never asked how it was for her. Not the first time, not any time after.

Because he'd never really cared about her.

"I…" She took a deep breath. "Actually, it was amazing." She didn't feel that was strong enough, so she rephrased. "You were amazing."

He stroked his thumb over her knuckles and she could tell he was smiling. But several seconds passed and he said, "But…"

He was asking. At the very least, she owed him her honesty. "I can't stay with you. I can't put my hopes and dreams into a future that I can't be sure will actually exist tomorrow."

He thought about that for a while. "I won't play with you, Tammy. That's not how I am."

Oh, hell—she was hurting his feelings. "I know," she said quickly. "And even if it does sound lame, it's the truth—it's not you. It's me. It's not that I don't take you at your word."

"Then what is it?"

"I just—look, I just need to stay in the now. One day at a time. Mikey has to come first and what happens between us…"

He kissed her hand again, but didn't say anything.

"I was selfish once," she heard herself say in a whisper. "I was selfish and stupid and I have to get up every single day and face that fact. And I love him *so* much—I didn't know I could love another person like I love my son. He's an amazing kid, you know? But…" She took a deep breath. "I can't afford to be selfish again. Not even for someone as good as you."

"I see." But he didn't release her hand, didn't tell

her to get a move on. He just sat there. She couldn't tell if that was a good thing or not. "And this today—this was selfish?"

"I don't know," she admitted. "I wanted you. I still want you." That was the truth of it. She wanted him and yet, she felt like she didn't deserve him.

He chuckled. "Well, that's a relief."

She tried to smile, but she didn't do an awesome job.

"So," he went on, sounding lighter. "The sex was okay—"

"Amazing," she corrected, her face growing hot.

"Agreed. Amazing. The part where I went wrong was... not staying in the present?"

"I guess that's it." She felt ridiculous when he put it like that. "That and the stretch marks." She tried to laugh. "They're just so... ugly."

This time, he didn't just kiss her hand. He leaned over and kissed her lips and all the glorious warmth flowed between them again. "You are beautiful. I don't want to hear you down on yourself again, okay?"

"Okay," she said. It came out soft and even a little weak.

"You're going to have to leave soon," he said, staring into her eyes. "But we still have a little time *now*."

She couldn't keep the smile off her face. "Yes," she agreed. This time, she was the one to stand and pull him into her. "I think we do."

Chapter Seven

Somehow, a month passed—one of the best months in Tammy's memory.

Every Saturday, she had lunch with Clarence and then they spent the rest of the afternoon wrapped around each other in bed. After a few weeks, she let him go down on her, which was a new experience—and a mind-blowing one.

Quickly, being with each other once a week became not enough. So they started having dinner every Wednesday night, as well. After the first dinner, Clarence insisted she bring Mikey the next time, so she did.

Clarence had a small present—a toy Thomas train and a DVD of Thomas stories to go with it and that was all it took for Mikey to decide that Clarence was just the coolest dude he'd ever known.

Then, one Friday night, Clarence came to dinner at the Tall Trees house. Tammy's mom was positively giddy to have "Tammy's friend" over and went so far as to bake a cake—which never happened outside of a birthday. Mikey told everyone—loudly—about all the cool stuff Clarence had given him or had at his house. The whole thing was all kinds of mortifying for Tammy, but at least Tara kept her mouth shut.

And, after Tammy had put Mikey to bed, she went home with Clarence and spent the night in his bed. And most of the morning there, too.

It was something she could get used to. Hell, it *was* something she was getting used to. Clarence didn't make any grand promises, nor did he ask them of her. The most they discussed the future was the next time they'd see each other. The next night they had dinner together, the next weekend afternoon they could spend together—even just the next morning at the Child Care Center, sitting on the couch, drinking coffee and occasionally kissing when Mikey wasn't paying attention.

There was no future, beyond tomorrow or this weekend or next week. There was just the now. And the now was pretty damn good.

In fact, the now was so good that Tammy had begun to allow herself to think beyond the next seven days because she'd been right about something— Clarence was a man she could love. He was constant and steady and responsible and she'd come to a place in her life where those things counted for a lot. But it wasn't just that, not when he laid her out on his bed and always, *always* made sure she came first.

She'd always remembered Ezra as being this special lover, how he'd awakened her to the joys of sex and how it hadn't been quite worth the surprise pregnancy and subsequent dumping but it was all she'd known and that made it special.

Now she knew better.

Ezra had been a selfish boy. Clarence? He put her first. He treated her son well. He made her want something more. He was a good man, possibly the best she'd ever known. And she was falling for him more and more each day.

"Maybe," she said one Saturday afternoon as she lay naked in his arms, both of them still breathing hard from the sex that got better every single time, "maybe we should start to think about… the not now."

Clarence propped himself up on his elbow and looked down at her. Hope burned bright in his eyes. "Yeah?"

"Maybe," she replied, feeling nervous. "Just a thought."

He looked like he wanted to smile but was trying really hard to not. "You mean like—and I'm just thinking out loud here—Halloween and Thanksgiving and Christmas? That's only two months of not now. I could take Mikey trick or treating and we could spend Christmas together."

"Yeah, okay." Two months ahead instead of two weeks ahead—that counted toward thinking about the future, right? "We can have Thanksgiving at my place, Christmas at yours?"

Then he did grin down at her. She did that—she made him happy like that. It still felt like a foreign idea, that she could be enough for someone as good as Clarence.

He lowered himself back onto her. "I know what I'm hoping to unwrap on Christmas morning," he murmured as he kissed her breasts, his hands moving over her body again.

She laughed, gripping his hair as his mouth moved lower and lower until his tongue was covering her clit and the tension began to wind her up again.

As he patiently brought her to the verge of

another orgasm and then expertly pushed her over the edge, a new thought popped up in her head. *I love this man.* There was no 'could,' no 'falling for.' Just a fact that she was unequivocally realizing for the first time.

Christmas. She'd see how things went between now and Christmas. And then… the New Year was only another week away. A new year—a new start.

Then maybe they'd talk about something more.

For the first time in a very long time, Tammy was hopeful about the future.

***

Clarence lifted Rosie Two Horses out of her wheelchair and onto the exam table, where he could check the diabetic sores on her legs and get her cleaned up.

Mentally, he was planning his trip into Rapid City after work. It was Thursday—not one of the nights he usually had dinner with Tammy and he had to make good use of his time. He was going to look at diamond rings. Christmas was six weeks off and he probably had enough money saved up for a nice ring, but he didn't want to leave it to the last minute.

He hoped she'd say yes. He wanted to think she would—Halloween had gone off without a hitch, if he didn't count Mikey getting hopped up on Pixie Stixs and pinballing around until he hit his head and giving himself a nice goose egg. If they could just make it through Thanksgiving…

But despite all the good things—the good times they spent together, both alone and as a family with Mikey—Clarence was worried about the proposal. He was going to be forty in less than three months.

Yeah, that worried him because Tammy was so focused on staying in the here and now—what happened when she really considered the future? He was practically an old man. Would she want more kids? Would she decide that, good as Clarence might be for right now, maybe he wasn't the best choice for the future because he had such a head start on her?

That was the thought that kept him up at night. He wasn't young and he was actively not getting any younger. He wanted to be what she needed for both now and forever, but he didn't know if that was possible.

Only one way to find out. He was going to ask. And he was going to make damned sure he had a diamond in his hand when he did so.

Lost in thought and focused on his job, Clarence didn't see the guy walk into the clinic. But he heard it when Tara said, "What the hell are you doing here?" in her meanest voice, which was usually enough to stop everyone from angry patients to would-be criminals in their tracks. Anyone who got through Tara had to go through him—or Nobody, if Clarence had already gone home.

"One second," he said to Rosie as he ducked his head out through the dividing curtains. He didn't recognize the guy standing in front of Tara—medium height, thin build, shoulder-length black hair that looked as if it'd been cut short and since had grown out. The guy had on a green army-style jacket and what might be combat boots under his jeans.

But he didn't have that lean and hungry look that went with a junkie looking for a fix and the Clinic didn't exactly operate with a flush of cash. In other words, he didn't look dangerous—certainly not the kind of guy Clarence would have to set down the hard way. Maybe the kind of guy he'd have a beer with, one former military man with another, but that was it.

Clarence was on the verge of turning back to his patient when the guy said something to Tara and she all but exploded out of her chair. "No way in hell, Ezra."

All the warning bells went off in Clarence's head. Ezra? *The* Ezra—Tammy's old flame and Mikey's father? The *dickbag* himself—here, in the Clinic?

"You can't just waltz in here and—" Whatever else Tara had been about to say died as Clarence plowed his way over to the reception desk.

"Problem?" he demanded as he glowered at Ezra the dickbag. Yeah, the kid—and so help him, the guy really did look like a kid that hadn't finished growing up yet—probably had done a couple of tours. But Clarence had six inches and probably a hundred pounds on him. If there was a problem, Clarence was the solution.

"Hey. I'm looking for Tammy Tall Trees and she," he said, nodding at Tara, "doesn't feel like helping me out today. You know where she's at, buddy?"

Tara and Clarence shared a look, which was not something that happened every single day, but today? Yeah, today they were completely, totally, 100% on the same side.

He glanced at the clock. 1:37. Tammy was next door, putting kids down for a nap or doing the lunch dishes. "She's not here."

Ezra the dickbag's smile tightened. "Okay, yeah—got that. Do you know where she's at?"

Neither Clarence nor Tara responded.

73

At that moment, Melonie Mitchell stuck her head through and called out over the sound of a kid pitching an epic fit, "Wanda Bright Sky? Are you in here?" A woman with a hacking cough stood up and moved toward the door that divided the Clinic and the Child Care Center.

"Hey," Ezra said to Melonie, "I'm looking for Tammy Tall Trees. Do you—"

"She's putting the kids down," Melonie said without looking up as she held the door for Wanda. "I'll tell her you're looking for her. I'm so sorry, Wanda, but he's really upset…" Her voice trailed off as she led Wanda into the room.

Ezra turned back to where Clarence and Tara were. "Not here, huh?" He looked Clarence up and down. "You never did like me," he told Tara.

"That's where you're wrong," Tara snapped. "I didn't give a damn about you one way or the other until you knocked up my baby sister and then ran off like a dog with its tail tucked—"

"Yes?" Tammy's head poked through the door. "I'm Tammy." Her gaze met Clarence's and at first she smiled, all happy to see him.

They hadn't talked a lot about their pasts, beyond the fact that Ezra had made promises and not kept them. Clarence didn't know if he should just get a jump on things and punch Ezra or if that would be the wrong way to handle this situation. The best he could do was give a little shake of his head in warning.

In that moment, Ezra turned around. "Whoa— Tammy? What the hell happened to you?"

"Ezra?" Tammy froze in place, her eyes wide in shock.

It didn't last long, that frozen moment, mostly because Clarence had Ezra by the back of the neck and was bodily removing his sorry ass from the Clinic. "You will *not* talk to her that way," he managed to growl in Ezra's ear before he launched him across the dirt parking lot.

"Clarence!" Tammy appeared at his side.

"I won't have him talk to you like that," Clarence repeated, dusting his hands off as if he'd been touching something grimy. "He's got no right. I won't have it."

Then, to his surprise, Tammy rushed over to where Ezra was sprawled out on the hard-pack dirt. "Are you okay?"

"Jesus, what the hell is *his* problem?" Tammy helped Ezra to his feet and even went so far as to help straighten his jacket for him.

Clarence could not begin to process what he was seeing. Tara had been right about this, at least—Ezra was a dickbag. What kind of man would ask the mother of his child—a woman he hadn't seen in five damned years—about her weight? Just thinking about it made his blood boil.

And yet, Tammy was over there with Ezra, apologizing for Clarence's behavior and generally being... nice? What the ever-loving hell? "I'm so sorry," she was saying as she fixed his freaking collar. "Are you all right?"

"Um, Tammy?" That was as far as he got. He wanted to do a whole lot more than just throw Ezra but that seemed to be a not-good plan at the moment.

She threw him a warning glance. "Well," she said in a too bright tone. "Ezra Johnson, this is Clarence

Thunder. Clarence," she went on as if this were a cocktail party and not a near brawl, "This is Ezra Johnson, Mikey's father."

"Yeah, we met," Ezra said, not offering his hand or anything. Not that Clarence would have shaken it anyway.

"Ezra," Tammy began in a tone that Clarence recognized as the one she used on kids who were spiraling out of control. "What are you doing here?"

"What—aren't you happy to see me?" he asked, keeping a wary eye on Clarence.

Yeah, buddy, Clarence thought. *You* should *be worried.* He flexed his shoulders.

"It's just—it's been a long time. If you were going to stop by, you could have called. I don't—this will be—I didn't have the chance to prepare Mikey, that's all," she said, stumbling over her words.

In that moment, Clarence didn't regret throwing the rat out. In fact, he'd really enjoy another chance to do it again because once again, Ezra was making Tammy's life harder simply by existing.

He cracked his knuckles in warning.

"You call him Mikey? That's—" He caught the movement of Clarence taking a step toward him.

Say something about the boy, Clarence mentally challenged him. *Say one thing.*

"Yeah, okay there, man. That's fine, okay?" Ezra took a step back, putting Tammy in between him and Clarence.

Clarence smiled. He had the upper hand here, even if he was almost old enough to be Ezra's dad.

Which left him completely unprepared for when Tammy turned around and glared at him. "Clarence," she said and he heard the nice tone start to fray. "Do you mind?"

"Yeah, actually, I do. A lot. You want me to get rid of him for you?"

"*Clarence.* I can handle this." Behind her, Ezra gave Clarence a bratty look.

Clarence grabbed Tammy and pulled her aside. "Babe," he said, pleading with her. "I don't want him to jerk you around—you or Mikey."

A look of doubt crossed her face. "I know, but he *is* Mikey's father."

"I don't want him to hurt you again," Clarence said, taking her hand in his. "I don't want him to mess things up." Things like engagement rings and wedding nights and growing old together. It was one thing if Tammy decided of her own free will that Clarence was already too old to spend the rest of her life with—but if Ezra somehow made it that Clarence shouldn't be around Mikey—well, Tammy had made it plain. The boy had to come first.

She managed to curve her mouth into a strained smile, but then Ezra snorted behind them as if he could not believe what he was seeing.

"That's *it*," Clarence growled as he made a move toward Ezra.

"No!" Tammy shouted, but that's not what stopped him.

"Mommy? Cwarence?" The sound of Mikey's small voice cutting through the air caused all the adults to freeze. "What's wrong?"

Chapter Eight

N othing, baby," Tammy said, giving both Ezra a warning glare and pushing Clarence back. "Behave," she hissed under her breath as Mikey looked from man to man, worry already making his lower lip tremble.

She hurried over and swept her boy into her arms. "Mikey, honey," she said, knowing that she had to be the grown-up here—especially since Clarence seemed to have suddenly reverted back to being a headstrong teenager.

This was not how she wanted this to go. For years, she'd dreamed of Ezra coming back. In those early fantasies, often the product of sleepless nights and teething, Ezra would have realized the errors of his ways and come crawling back, begging her forgiveness for being such an ass. He'd propose and mean it this time and then, finally, they'd live happily ever after.

Maybe about the time Mikey had turned two, though, those dreams had faded under the crushing weight of reality. Ezra was not going to come crawling back. There would be no fairy-tale wedding and no happy ending. Not for her.

At least, not until Clarence.

She took a deep breath. She had to be strong for Mikey. "This is Ezra, baby. This is your daddy."

"Hey there, squirt," Ezra said.

Tammy forced herself not to glare at Ezra. How had she ever though she'd loved him? Despite the years that had passed, he still had a childish, almost sullen, attitude that she'd once thought was the height of cool and now she recognized as sheer immaturity.

And just like that, she felt foolish all over again. She'd fallen for *that*? Really?

Mikey, God bless his little heart, managed a perfectly polite, "Hi," before burying his face in Tammy's neck.

"Aren't you glad to see your dad?" Ezra asked and for the first time, Tammy heard something else in his tone—hurt, maybe. As if he'd envisioned being this knight in shining armor, welcomed back with open and loving arms.

As if Tammy really wouldn't have moved on with her life.

"I want Cwarence," Mikey whispered into her hair, so quietly that she was sure no one else had heard her.

Her heart broke in ways she didn't think were still possible. "I know, honey," she whispered back. Then, in her best keep-calm-and-be-the-grown-up voice, she said, "It's almost his nap time, Ezra." She gritted her teeth. She knew what she had to do, but she wished that she didn't have Clarence looming over her shoulder.

She didn't know he could be like this—so physically intimidating, so danged *mean*. Yes, she realized he was a massive tank of a man—hard to miss that when she was sleeping with him—but when he was with her, he was respectful and mindful and always put her first.

Now? Now she'd seen him pick Ezra up, seemingly by the back of his neck, and physically throw him out of the clinic. And if Ezra said one more less-than-flattering thing to her, she didn't have much doubt that Clarence would pound Ezra into the dirt.

There was no way to make everyone happy here. So she did what she had to. "Ezra, maybe you can come to dinner tonight? Mikey will be up from his nap by then."

Clarence growled behind her. She felt him move and tensed—she really didn't want to have to hold him back while she had Mikey in his arms.

Mikey, for his part, shook his little head back and forth in silent protest. God, she hated doing this. But the boy should know his father.

Shouldn't he?

"*He* going to be there?" Ezra asked with a jerk of his chin toward Clarence.

"No," Tammy said at the exact same moment Clarence said, "Yes."

The door to the Clinic opened behind her. "I hate to interrupt," said a tight female voice that could only belong to one woman—Dr. Madeline Mitchell. "Clarence, we have patients waiting. If there's a problem, call Tim or Rebel."

Tammy cringed. She could imagine that Tara had probably already called Tim, the sheriff, just because Ezra existed. "I have to get back to work, too," Tammy said, mostly because she didn't want to be alone with Ezra, knowing that everyone in the Clinic would be watching and also because it was true. She was still on the clock and Melonie might cut her some slack, but getting all the kids down for naptime was a two-woman job.

There was a moment of tense silence and she could feel Clarence glaring at Ezra. For his part, Ezra had an eat-shit-and-die grin on his face that she'd once thought was such a bad-boy look.

"Watch yourself around her," was what Clarence said. Then he was gone, stomping back to the clinic with enough force to make the ground shake.

Mikey whimpered against her neck. "I'm sorry," she said to Ezra again. But then it hit her—why the hell was she apologizing to him? He was the one who'd left the first time. He was the one who'd broken his promise to her. And now he was the one who'd rolled in here without a single thought as to how this might upset Mikey?

Now, without Clarence being angry behind her, she could feel the force of her own rage starting to build. "Actually," she said, when Ezra took a step forward, like she was somehow the safer of the two options, "I'm not that sorry. Why didn't you call, at least? You can't show up after five years and expect to us to fall all over ourselves to accommodate you."

Mikey's grip tightened around her neck. *Sorry, honey*, she thought, rubbing his back. But suddenly she had to do this—had to show him that she wasn't just waiting on him—that he'd never be her knight in shining armor.

"You sound like your sister," Ezra stated flatly.

"Did it ever occur to you that she might be right? You left me. You left *us*, Ezra. Do you even have an excuse for that? Or was it just cowardice?"

"I wasn't a coward," he snapped. "I joined the Army. I did two tours in Afghanistan. I'm a warrior. Unlike your 'friend' there," he added, using air quotes, as if Clarence could be diminished by this opinion of him.

"My 'friend' is my boyfriend, Ezra. And he was in the Navy for ten years. He's a good man who takes care of people. Of *us*," she added, hugging Mikey tightly. "So, if I were you, I'd think twice about mocking the best man on this rez. He's already thrown you out once."

Mikey started to cry. Tammy did not get upset very often and she felt bad for losing her temper right now in front of him but she'd always dreamed of what she might say to Ezra if he ever came back.

Funny, this was not how she'd thought it'd go.

"I need to get back to work," she repeated. "If you'd like to come to dinner, you're welcome. Your son is an amazing boy and he should know you. But if you thought that you could just roll back onto this rez and we'd be here waiting with open arms, well, I'm sorry. I put my son first."

Ezra stared at her as if he'd never seen her before. Tammy certainly felt like it. She wasn't the same naïve, hopeful girl she'd been. It wasn't that she was older, although she was. But she'd fought her own battles, her own personal war between poverty and single motherhood and she'd made it as best she could without him.

"I thought you'd be glad to see me," he said in a quiet voice. "I thought…"

"You thought wrong." She took a deep breath, still rubbing Mikey's back. "I still live with my mom. And Tara," she added, figuring she owed him at least that much warning. When he made a face of disdain, she told him, "I couldn't afford my own place once I had Mikey," because that was his fault, too.

If only he'd stayed...

Well, then she'd be stuck with him. Saddled with a resentful, immature boy-man who didn't know how to be a father or a good lover.

"Come by for dinner." She knew it'd be a disaster one way or the other. If Clarence showed up, Tammy would spend the whole time making sure the two men didn't fight like toddlers over a favorite toy. And even if Clarence stayed home, Tara would be in super-bitch mode.

"Yeah." He rubbed the back of his neck. "Okay."

Tammy watched as he turned, got into a rusted-out Jeep and drove off.

"Honey, I'm sorry," Tammy said in a soothing voice as she watched Ezra drive away.

Would he show up for dinner tonight? Or would he bail again?

Either way, she was going to be sorry.

***

Clarence did not watch Ezra and Tammy through the door. Dr. Mitchell was giving him *the look*, patients were piling up, and besides, Tara was doing plenty of watching and adding color commentary to her play-by-play.

"He's turning," she announced as Clarence tried to focus on taking an older man's blood pressure. "He's getting in his car—what a piece of junk!— and—okay, he's gone."

The whole Clinic seemed to breathe a sigh of relief at that. "Women," the older patient said with a sympathetic nod of his head. "Yours?"

"Yeah," Clarence muttered, trying once again to keep count of the beats per minute and failing.

"Women," the man said again. "But then again, they're worth it, eh?"

Clarence tried to smile at the old coot, but his head was a swirling mess. Why hadn't he ever thought about what might happen if Mikey's dad came back? Why hadn't he thought about how Tammy might rush to defend the jerk because, after all, he *was* Mikey's dad?

She hadn't even wanted him to come to dinner. And damn it all, he had to respect that wish even if it felt wrong—even if he knew he should be there to back her up and make sure Ezra didn't start making snide comments about her body or her son—because he'd made a promise to her that he would respect her wishes.

Even the wish where he didn't get to beat that smarmy little jerk into an oil stain. Dammit.

What made it worse was that Tammy didn't come over on her way out. Not that she normally did—she was usually trying to get Mikey home before he fell asleep for naptime and, anyway, they didn't want everyone looking at them. Yeah, most people had gathered there was something going on between them—it wasn't a secret—but they didn't fool around at work. At least, not once other people were present.

Still, when Tammy didn't even stick her head through the divider and tell him what she and Ezra had agreed upon, it bothered him. No, Clarence wasn't the boy's father and maybe he didn't have a vote in this matter. But he'd given the kid toys and had a small-but-growing DVD collection of cartoons with talking animals and trains at his house and he'd taken the boy trick-or-treating and that had to count for something, didn't it? He was in love with Mikey's mom and if they got married, he'd be Mikey's stepfather and didn't that mean he at least got to have a say?

Unless…

Unless he wasn't going to get the chance to be Mikey's stepfather.

Tammy took her son home without stopping to see Clarence. And she did not want him to come to dinner that night. She'd been plenty plain about that.

Hell.

Maybe he shouldn't go look at rings tonight after all.

Chapter Nine

Mom was not happy when Tammy told her that Ezra might be stopping by to see Mikey. "The one who left you high and dry? *That* no-good bum?"

"Mom," Tammy said in a warning tone as Mikey began fuss. Yes, Ezra was a jerk and yes, Mikey had probably heard Tara call him a dickbag on numerous occasions. But that had been back when 'daddy' was an abstract idea, not a real person who was coming to dinner. "Can we try not to bad-mouth him in front of the kids?"

Mom gave her a look that was part glare, part confusion. "Fine," she said. "I'll set another place at the table. But I don't have to like it."

"Thanks." Mikey sat down on the floor and started to cry in earnest. "I need to try and get him to go down in case…"

As irritated as her mother was, the older woman nodded. "Go on," she said with the same put-upon sigh she'd heaved all those years ago when Tammy had revealed she was pregnant, as if this were just another inevitable trial to suffer through.

Tammy lifted Mikey up and carried him back to the room they shared. Back when he'd been a baby and Tammy had been unemployed, she'd napped with him a lot. He seemed to sleep better with her next to him. But in the last year or so, she'd come to value that quiet time more than the extra sleep. Besides, the boy turned like a top when he was dreaming and she got kicked enough at night.

Today, she lay down with him. He was still so upset by the afternoon's events that he was whimpering quietly, a tight, pained little noise from the back of his throat. The noise seemed to punch right through her. It'd been bad enough when Ezra had hurt her. Mikey hadn't been a factor then, other than an unknown baby that was ruining everything.

But now Mikey was a solid, real human who was fully capable of feeling the sting of rejection even if he couldn't understand why.

She'd take his pain away if she could, but she knew she couldn't do much more than calm him down because she might never understand the *why*, either.

"Baby," she whispered as she rubbed his back. "It's okay." She hoped he couldn't tell that she didn't quite believe it herself.

"But, Mommy—that was my daddy?"

"Yes, honey." She sighed—and then hoped it wasn't the same world-weary sigh of her mom. The last thing she needed today was to turn into her mother. "I loved him very much once, but then he had to go away. He joined the army."

"He left us," Mikey said, tears spilling down his cheeks.

Tammy winced to hear her words coming out of her son's mouth. "I know, honey. But we did okay. You have me and Aunt Tara and Grandma and... and Clarence." Mikey gave her a look of uncertainty. "And if Daddy comes over tonight—" She couldn't bring herself to say when because she couldn't bring herself to put any stock in a promise that Ezra Johnson made, not even a small one about dinner. "Well, if he comes over we'll just... get to know him. You should know your daddy," she added, sounding more sure than she felt. "He'll always be your daddy, even if he's not always here."

That was the best promise she could make him. It wasn't fair to ask a four year old to understand a concept as foreign as that, but he was going to learn that one way or the other.

Mikey yawned and stuck his thumb in his mouth. Tammy thought he might nod off but then he said, "Will Cwarence be here?"

"I don't know, honey. This isn't his regular night," she half-lied. Because he'd said he'd be here in such a way that made it pretty damn clear that wild horses wouldn't keep him away.

But then, at the same time, she'd said *no*, he was not coming over. The talk in the parking lot had been tense enough and as much of a coward as Ezra was— warrior or no—he deserved a chance to get to know his son without Clarence sitting in judgment of him.

Mikey's eyes began to drift shut. "If you marry Cwarence, will he be my daddy, too? He'd be a good daddy." The last part came out as a barely intelligible mumble.

Tammy's heart began to pound. If she married Clarence? "Let's take a nap," she said in her calmest voice when she felt anything but calm. "Love you, honey."

"Love you, Mommy." And then, miracle of miracle, Mikey closed his eyes and started to breath regularly.

Tammy lay there, watching her son sleep. Would Ezra show up tonight? She wanted to think he would, that he'd seen the light and wanted to get to know his son and maybe even be a part of his life.

But she didn't think so. Something in the way he'd said, "Yeah, okay," when she'd told him to come to dinner…

She'd seen that cornered look in his eyes before, five years ago, when she'd told him she was pregnant and scared and he'd made that final promise to her. "I'll take care of you, babe," he'd said. The words had sounded great—the very thing she needed to hear—but it'd been the way he said it, rubbing the back of his neck as he backed away from her.

She wanted to be over the pain of abandonment but seeing him again today and knowing, deep down inside, that he was the same boy he'd been before…

When she was sure Mikey was asleep, she slipped out of their room and went to the phone. She called the Clinic. She'd tell Clarence she'd changed her mind, that he should be here tonight because if Ezra didn't show and Clarence wasn't here, she wasn't sure she could keep Mikey from losing it. She wasn't sure she wouldn't lose it.

"Clinic," Tara answered.

"It's me," Tammy replied. "Is Clarence there?"

"What did you say to that dickbag? Please tell me you told him to go to hell, Tammy. *Please*."

Tammy sighed. Her sister could carry a grudge like nobody's business. "I invited him over for dinner."

"You *what*?" Tara gasped in true horror. "How could you?"

89

"He's Mikey's father," Tammy replied as patiently as she could. "And if you could please not call him a dickbag in front of Mikey, that'd be great."

"You're not seriously thinking of taking him back, are you? Tammy, I thought you were smarter than that!"

"Tara," Tammy snapped. "I'm not. This is about Mikey, not me. I want to talk to Clarence. Please."

"Well, he's not here. He cut out early, said he had something to do. Is he coming over for dinner tonight, too? Gosh," Tara said sarcastically, "this is going to be all kinds of fun, isn't it?"

Another spike of terror hit her in the stomach. Clarence did not cut out early. He was reliable and trustworthy and not the kind who just up and disappeared.

And she'd never seen him as mad as he'd been when he'd thrown Ezra out. Oh, God. "Did he say where he was going?"

"Nope. But I have to tell you, him kicking Ezra out was the highlight of my week."

"Yeah, thanks," Tammy said as she hung up. She dialed Clarence's home. No answer.

This was not like him. They'd gotten to a point where she knew his schedule and he knew hers. Neither of them had a habit of disappearing—which was something she liked about him. She'd had enough of boyfriends vanishing off into the night. Knowing where Clarence was and when, more or less, was a comfort.

So for him to suddenly vanish like this—it couldn't be a coincidence. He wouldn't have gone looking for Ezra, would he?

She dialed his number again and let it ring. *Pick up*, she thought. *Please pick up. Please still be there.*

He didn't.

She stared at the phone. This was not the same thing, she tried to tell herself. It'd been a bad day for everyone and Clarence probably just needed... some time to think, that was all.

She'd been wrong to say he shouldn't come tonight, she knew that now. She'd been trying to keep the peace at the time... but now that she'd thought about it, she *knew* she needed him by her side.

Where *was* he?

And then there was Mikey, asking if she was going to marry Clarence and if Clarence would be his daddy.

She'd known this would happen, after all. Clarence had been wonderful to her and to Mikey and she'd fallen in love with him. She'd risked her heart, which was one thing, but Mikey...

Mikey loved Clarence, too. And Clarence didn't seem to mind that the boy was another man's child. He got Mikey thoughtful little presents and made sure that he was taken care of when the three of them were together and seemed to enjoy the silliness that went hand in hand with a four year old. And all of that had made Tammy love him more.

Maybe she'd call again, just to be sure.

But no. Clarence did not answer the phone.

Once again, she was on her own. How disappointing.

Luckily, she was used to it.

***

Clarence was not, as a rule, a real spiritual guy. He didn't sit in sweat lodges and talk to spirits, nor did he attend Sunday services with any regularity. He'd seen too much war and pain and suffering to put a hell of a lot of stock into Higher Powers and gods and God.

Which did not explain why he was driving out to see a medicine man during working hours, except he had no other good options at this point.

Besides, going to talk to Rebel Runs Fast wasn't exactly a religious experience. Clarence was sure that, if he wanted to go into a sweat lodge, Rebel would start heating the rocks. And the man would be happy to discuss any visions Clarence may or may not have.

But that's not why Clarence was here.

He'd bailed on work early, which made him feel lousy, so that he could talk to Rebel before his wife—and Clarence's boss—Dr. Mitchell, got home from work.

If he didn't know Rebel so well, Clarence might have been surprised to see the man sitting around a campfire, despite the fall chill in the air that went with earlier and earlier sunsets. But Rebel had a way of knowing when someone was on the way to see him. What did surprise Clarence was that Nobody Bodine was also sitting at the fire.

Nobody was the night janitor at the Clinic and he did a good job, but the man was little more than a vigilante with an underdeveloped moral compass. It wasn't that the men who had the misfortune of meeting Nobody Bodine in the shadows of the night didn't deserve what they got—they were often men who sold drugs or beat children or worse. Clarence would know—he'd sewn more than his share of bad men back together.

But Clarence was a Navy man. He liked his order and he liked his rules. Shipshape and Bristol fashion, as his old commander used to say. And Nobody didn't follow either directive.

"Hiya," Rebel said as he added more wood to the fire.

"Hiya, Rebel. Nobody," Clarence added, just to be polite. He didn't often see Nobody—the man was a shadow. Even now, it was hard to resist taking a long look at the man some people believed was really a ghost.

But when he focused on Nobody the shadows seemed to… bend toward him, like it was darker where he sat. He nodded at Clarence.

Clarence sat on the far side of the fire from Nobody. No one spoke for a few minutes as Rebel got the fire blazing enough that it put out some actual heat.

Clarence knew he needed to get talking—he only had so much time before Dr. Mitchell got home—or, for that matter, Melonie Mitchell came looking for Nobody. Or worse, both sisters showed up together. Clarence wasn't sure he could handle that level of feminine onslaught right now.

But there was something about the flames that pulled him in. The fire wasn't—well, it wasn't like watching television. No shapes formed and acted out a scene from his past, present, or future. But there was *something* about the way the fire flickered back and forth that didn't seem like a regular fire burning a regular log. That something made him think of his first year in the Navy, of being a young punk who was scared shitless by all that water but who was desperate to get off the rez and do something with his life.

He didn't know how long he sat there, watching

the red dance with the orange, so when Rebel said, "I heard Ezra Johnson was back," it made Clarence jump.

He shook back to himself and whatever'd been in the flames seemed to go up in smoke. "Yeah. He showed up at the Clinic today."

Rebel chuckled. "And you threw him out just for that?"

He shouldn't be surprised. This was not a matter of Rebel and his habit of having 'visions.' Everyone on this entire rez probably knew about the almost-fight today. "He said things he shouldn't have said to Tammy and I wasn't going to stand for it."

Nobody snorted in appreciation of this, which did not make Clarence feel a hell of a lot better because picking Ezra up and giving him the old heave-ho was exactly the kind of thing Nobody would have done.

Rebel grinned at the fire, as if the something that might or might not be there was clearer to him than it was to Clarence. "And that explains why you're here, then? Not that it's not great to see you and all."

Clarence sighed. "She told Ezra to come to dinner and me not to. She didn't want me there."

"You did throw the man out," Rebel pointed out.

"He deserved it. Left her high and dry for years and the first thing out of his mouth when he sees her isn't an apology—it's a crack about her body? *No.*" And just like that, Clarence wanted to throw that dickbag across the threshold all over again. He deserved that and more for what he'd done to Tammy.

Which, to be honest, was the reason Clarence had been forcibly un-invited from dinner.

"And…" Rebel said, as if the all-seeing Rebel Runs Fast wasn't actually sure why Clarence was here.

He didn't really want to have this conversation with Nobody. But he didn't have a choice, as the shadow wasn't moving from where he sat. "She told me, back at the beginning, that she didn't want to talk about the future. Just the now, that's what she said. Didn't want to plan ahead, didn't want to get her hopes up."

"Understandable," Rebel said agreeably, his gaze still fastened on the flames. "But…"

"I was going to ask her to marry me. At Christmas." He'd been counting down the days with the kind of excitement that hadn't possessed him since he was six. How many more days until Christmas? How many more days until he could propose? Until he could move Tammy and Mikey into his house? Until he could get on with the rest of his life, a family by his side and a good woman in his bed?

"Excellent idea," Rebel agreed. Clarence glanced at Nobody, who nodded. "So what's the problem?"

"That dick—I mean, Ezra. I didn't… I didn't plan on him. On her defending him. I can't—I mean, I'm an old man. And if he comes back, if he decides he wants her back and he'll do what it takes—I can't compete with that. He's Mikey's dad. I'm just… nothing."

A silence that pained him settled around them because what could Rebel or even Nobody say to that? Those were the cold, hard facts. Clarence had known it from the beginning—he was too old for her and there was no way he could win a battle for her heart against a younger man she already was tied to through Mikey.

"Ask her." The sound of Nobody actually talking—out loud—made Clarence jump again.

"What?" Had he ever heard Nobody talk before?

"Ask her," he repeated, as if that were all Clarence needed to know.

"He's right," Rebel agreed. "Ask her anyway. You're only, what—forty?"

"Forty in three months," he replied. Ask her anyway? After his behavior today? Yeah, he hadn't done himself any favors there.

Rebel started to laugh and even Nobody cracked a smile. "Shit, man. That isn't old. Not when you can still haul a man's ass and shot-put it across a parking lot. You've got a claim. Stake it." He turned a kind smile to Clarence. "Don't be a dick. It's really that simple."

What the hell was that supposed to mean? "Yeah, okay." He looked over at Nobody—but the man was gone. Seconds later, headlights cut through the dusk from far down the road. Dr. Mitchell was almost home.

"You better go," Rebel said. "She's not too happy with you right now."

"Can't blame her." After all, getting into a fight and then bailing before his time was up was kind of a dick move. "See you," he said as he hurried to his car.

He passed Dr. Mitchell on the road and was unsurprised when she glared at him. He gave an apologetic shrug of his shoulders and then drove on.

Ask her anyway? Don't be a dick. How was that simple? Rebel was usually better with the advice thing than that. He didn't leave things unfinished—

Then realization hit Clarence so hard that he almost drove off the road.

Don't be a dick.

Like that dickbag had been.

Oh, hell—he had to get to Tammy right *now*.

Chapter Ten

Of course Ezra didn't show. That part didn't really surprise Tammy any more than it surprised her mom and Tara. The only person who had the capacity to be upset by this development was Mikey and he was going to make them all pay for his daddy not being there yet again.

When Mom said, "Dinner's ready," Mikey insisted that they wait for Ezra. After fifteen minutes, Tammy was forced to say they should eat without Ezra, which was not what Mikey wanted to hear. Raging with a fury that only a four-year-old boy was capable of maintaining, he threw his toys, nearly hitting the T.V. with a toy car and clocking his cousin Nelly in the head with a stuffed animal. Tammy had to wrap him up with both her arms and legs to keep him from breaking something. She just held him while he sobbed and she cried, too.

Of course Ezra hadn't come. She'd expected that, expected the tantrum Mikey would throw at having his world knocked out from under him.

"I want Cwarence," he wept at one point.

"Me, too, honey. Me, too."

She hadn't expected Clarence to abandon her. And that was what hurt.

Eventually—after about an hour—Mikey calmed down enough that she could release him from her python-like full-body hold. He refused to eat any of the dinner that Mom had saved for him. No one tried to push it. No one wanted another round of hysterics. So Tammy helped him get into his jammies and put him back to bed. She didn't even argue about brushing his teeth. They'd start over—again—tomorrow.

She was reading Goodnight, Moon to him when she heard it—a knock at the door. She tried not to react—Mikey was calm—but she tensed. The boy shot up in bed. "Who's here?" he demanded, already fully awake.

"Honey, I don't know," she told him. Ezra? Clarence? Someone else? "But I'll find out," she promised. "You stay here. You're supposed to be going to sleep."

She hurried out as calmly as she could. She wouldn't get her hopes up one way or the other. She would not.

But then she saw Clarence standing there, his brow furrowed with worry as Mom and Tara stared at him as if he were a buffalo that had wandered into the living room. No, not even a buffalo. Something rarer—like a wooly mammoth.

He was here. He'd come back. Oh, God. Please don't let this be a dream, she thought, because if she'd fallen asleep while reading to Mikey and this wasn't real, she wasn't sure she could take another loss, even one that only happened in her mind.

Tammy must have made a noise when she saw him there because he looked up and everything about his face changed into a mix of regret and fear and need. "Clarence!"

"I missed dinner," he said in a soft voice, like he was afraid he'd spook her. "Sorry about that. I wasn't sure if you wanted me here or not."

"It's okay." Which wasn't true, of course. "I tried to call you, but you weren't home."

"I know." He opened his mouth to say something else, but then a small, Spiderman-clad ball of energy came flying out of the bedroom and launched at Clarence.

"Where were you? Daddy didn't come and I was sad," Mikey said in as scolding a tone as he could pull off while smiling. "And Mommy was sad, too."

"Hey, little man," Clarence said as he swooped Mikey up into his arms and hugged the boy. "I got here as soon as I could. Didn't want you or your mom to be sad."

Even though he didn't say the words to her, the sentiment still managed to put a small smile on her face. He *had* been thinking of her.

But more than that, he'd come back.

Mikey hugged him back. Tears started to prick at Tammy's eyes. Mom sniffed and even Tara seemed to be touched.

"I have to talk to your mom some more," Clarence said, setting Mikey down. "You need to go to sleep, okay?"

Mikey gave him a stern look even as he was still clinging to Clarence's hand. "You're not going to leave us, are you?"

"No, son, I'm not."

Son. It was the sort of thing a father might say to his child. Her heart tightened. If only...

Then Clarence appeared to realize that this exchange was taking place in front of the entire household. He patted Mikey on the head and said to Tammy, "Can I talk to you?"

Tammy shot a look to Mom, who got the hint faster than Tara. "Come on, sweetie, I'll read you another story." She picked up Mikey and carried him back to the bedroom.

Tara lingered a moment longer before she headed back to her room with a superior look. Clarence rolled his eyes and then smiled at Tammy. Yeah, they both still had to deal with Tara come tomorrow morning.

Then they were alone. Tammy wasn't sure what she wanted to say at this point. Yes, it was wonderful that he'd come back. But he'd left her hanging for a few hours and she was drained from dealing with Mikey and Ezra and the whole stinking mess. She didn't know if she was mad at him or thankful or what. All of the above, more than likely, and that was hard to put into words.

Suddenly, Clarence moved. He closed the distance between them in two massive steps, grabbed her by the shoulders and kissed the hell out of her.

Tammy was so surprised at first that she jerked her head up and caught his nose on hers. But then he pulled her into his chest and held her tight. She relaxed into his embrace. He'd come back for them. For *her*.

"I wasn't trying to run away—not from you," he said when the kiss ended. "I just—well, I had to think." He gave her a sad sort-of smile as he cupped her cheek in his palm. "I shouldn't have disappeared. I'm sorry. I would have been here sooner, but…"

"I was worried about you," she told him. She touched the lines on his forehead. "Mikey was so upset and then Ezra didn't show and you weren't here and I felt…"

100

"Alone. I know. And I know Ezra is a part of your life and of Mikey's whether he's here or not."

She rested her head against his chest. "I don't want you to disappear. I know I might not have the right to ask that of you, but I don't want you to go away. Not like tonight, not like Ezra did." She knew she could survive on her own—well, with the help of her sister and mother, that was—but she didn't want to be alone again. Not even for an evening.

He tilted her head back and gave her a small smile. "You know what I was going to do tonight, before it all went to hell in a handbasket?" She shook her head no. There was something in his eyes that was different—more serious. "I was going to go into town and do some Christmas shopping. But I don't think I can wait for Christmas anymore."

With that, he stepped back and dropped to his knees. Tammy's eyes went wide. "Clarence?"

He took her hands in his. Such large hands—they surrounded hers with their strength. "Will you marry me, Tammy Tall Trees?"

She gaped at him, too stunned to speak. Her thoughts were a jumble. Married? After today? Christmas?

After a long second, during which her brain refused to process, Clarence's confidence faltered. "I'll understand if the answer's no," he hurried to say. "I'm not a young man and—"

That was as far as he got before Tammy threw her arms around his neck and kissed the words out of his mouth. So she didn't have the words. Actions spoke louder.

He folded her into his arms again as he stood. "I'm not too old for you?"

"No, Clarence. You don't mind being a father to Mikey?"

"Naw, he's a great kid." He grinned down at her as if he wasn't sure if this were real or a dream. "You haven't answered the question yet."

She felt her own smile answering his. "You're everything I wanted but I didn't want to let myself hope. I'd hoped once and it'd blown up in my face. I didn't want to risk myself again. And tonight I was afraid maybe I'd hoped too much. I want you *so* much."

He hugged her harder than he'd ever hugged her before. "You're perfect for me, Tammy. I promise I'll never bail on you." He kissed her again, and this time it packed more heat. "Let me make coffee for you every single morning for the rest of our lives. I'm yours."

She started laughing and crying at the same time. To know that he'd be there for her—for their family— not just now, but forever. "Yes. *Yes*."

Then they went to tell Mikey, because the rest of their lives started right now.

About the Author

Award-winning author Sarah M. Anderson may live east of the Mississippi River, but her heart lies out west on the Great Plains. When she started writing, it wasn't long before her characters found themselves out in South Dakota among the Lakota Sioux. She loves to put people from two different worlds into new situations and see how their backgrounds and cultures take them someplace they never thought they'd go.

With over 1.2 million copies published in over twenty-one countries, Sarah has published over 40 books. Sarah's book *A Man of Privilege* won a RT Book Reviews 2012 Reviewers' Choice Best Book Award. *The Nanny Plan* was a 2016 RITA® winner for Best Contemporary: Short. Additionally, Sarah has given workshops at national and regional conferences, taught craft classes online, spoken at libraries and book clubs, and published articles in the Romance Writers Report. Find out more about Sarah's books at www.sarahmanderson.com. and sign up for the new-release newsletter at http://eepurl.com/nv39b.

Readers can find out more about Sarah's love of cowboys and Indians at:

Her Newsletter: http://eepurl.com/nv39b

Her Website: www.sarahmanderson.com

On Facebook: www.facebook.com/pages/Sarah-M-Anderson-Author

On Twitter: @SarahMAnderson1

On Goodreads: www.goodreads.com/author/show/4982413.Sarah_M_Anderson

By Snail Mail at: Sarah M. Anderson, 200 N 8th ST #193, Qincy IL 62301-9996

Other Books by Sarah M. Anderson

Men of the White Sandy
The Medicine Man
The Rancher
The Shadow
The Medic
The Sheriff
The Wannabe Cowboy

Lawyers in Love
A Man of His Word
A Man of Privilege
A Man of Distinction
Pride and Pregnancy

The Boltons
Straddling the Line
Bringing Home the Bachelor
Expecting a Bolton Baby
Little Secrets: Claiming His Pregnant Bride

Rich, Rugged Ranchers
A Real Cowboy

The Texas Cattleman's Club
What a Rancher Wants
His Lost and Found Family
A Surprise for the Sheikh

Dynasties: The Newports
Claimed by the Cowboy

Sarah M. Anderson

Rodeo Dreamers
Rodeo Dreams
One Rodeo Season
Crushing on the Cowboy

The First Family of Rodeo
His Best Friend's Sister
His Enemy's Daughter
His for One Night

The Beaumont Heirs
Not the Boss's Baby
Seduced by the Cowboy
A Beaumont Christmas Wedding
His Son, Her Secret
Falling for Her Fake Fiancé
His Illegitimate Heir
Rich Rancher for Christmas
Billionaire's Baby Promise

Billionaires and Babies
The Nanny Plan
His Forever Family
Twins for the Billionaire
Seduction on His Terms

Holiday Novellas
The Christmas Pony

NotMyFirstRodeo.com
Something About a Cowboy
Roping a Rancher

Writing as Maggie Chase
The Jeweled Ladies: The Mistress Series
His Topaz
Their Emerald
Her Ebony
His Sapphire
His Crown Jewel

The Jeweled Ladies: The Rogues Series
His Diamond
Their Amethyst

The Sheriff
(Men of the White Sandy #5)

© 2017 by Sarah M. Anderson

The last thing he needs is another person he has to protect…

Tim Means is the sheriff on the White Sandy Reservation—a thankless job on the best of days. He's trying to keep a gang war from breaking out, vigilantes from running amuck and he's doing it all with a two-man force. When a kid named Georgey gets busted breaking into the Clinic, Tim doesn't have time to keep the kid on the straight and narrow. He needs a relative to take the teen off his hands.

But who? The only person who could take custody of Georgey is Summer Collins, Georgey's half-sister. She hasn't been on the White Sandy in almost twelve years. But what choice does she have? She made a promise to her father to look out for her little brother, so she gives up her job teaching summer school and her hopes of a summer fling to venture west and meet a brother she barely remembers. But what she finds on the White Sandy is more than just a family or a sense of belonging. She meets one sexy sheriff and suddenly, a summer fling seems like just the thing.

But things on the White Sandy are never simple—or easy. When the gang war threatens Summer and her brother, will Tim be able to do his job—or will his heart get in the way?

Excerpt from *Sheriff Tim*

Just as she approached the T in the road—the T that had lead her down to a frightening dead-end, she saw the most wonderful thing ever—a cop car was approaching. Even better, it was slowing down! Dear God, please let it be someone on the White Sandy police force.

The car pulled off to the side of the road at the intersection. Summer's breath caught in her throat as she watched the man get out of the cop car. Was this the same man she talked to on the phone—Sheriff Means? Because the man striding toward her looked absolutely nothing like the man she pictured in her head.

Instead of short hair streaked with white, he had long black hair that came down just below his shoulders. It wasn't even tied back in a tail—instead, the breeze caught it and blew it around him. And the man she'd been picturing had had a gut—too much beer and too many donuts. But the man who was now walking around her car was lean and muscled and moved with a coiled grace that did more than catch her breath—he took it away.

He stood by the driver side door while she gaped

at him. She hadn't remembered much about her brief time on the reservation, but she remembered what her father had looked like. Actually, now that she thought about it, her father in the way she'd envisioned this officer looking work that different. Large and heavyset with short hair that was going white.

One corner of his mouth quirked up into what she hoped was an amused smile and he made a motion for her to roll down her window.

Oh, damn. She'd just been sitting there, staring at him. She quickly rolled down the window. "Sheriff Means?"

He nodded his head in acknowledgment. "Ms. Collins?"

"Yes. Call me Summer." She didn't know why she said that. She was Ms. Collins as all of her students called her. She was perfectly fine answering to her last name.

But for just a moment, she felt almost like someone else.

"Then you have to call me Tim," the sheriff said, his warm brown eyes doing something that looked remarkably like twinkling.

Was he laughing at her? Or was he flirting with her?

She jerked her gaze away from his face. Was it hot in here? "How did you know where I was?" She looked around at the nothingness that surrounded them. "I mean, I don't even know where I am and there's no one around. Except..." She looked in the rearview mirror that she didn't see that something that had been there earlier.

Sheriff Means—Tim—stiffened and turned to look back behind the car.

"What is it?" She asked, a bit of that panic coming back up. At least this time, she wasn't alone. She had an officer of the law—she glanced down and saw that he did have a gun at his side. An *armed* officer of the law. Whatever that shadow thing had been, she wouldn't be scared anymore.

Tim was scowling at the open space behind her car. "It's all right," he said in a comforting voice that he'd used during a phone call. "You saw something, I take it?"

She nodded, unsure she was supposed to feel silly for being scared of shadows or terrified that he knew what she'd seen.

"You have nothing to worry about," he went on, setting his hands on the roof of her car and leaning down closer. Tobacco—not cigarettes and not cigars but the good kind that she'd only smell during that one powwow—wafted around him and unconsciously, she leaned forward and inhaled deeply. "What you saw was a man—an...associate of mine, if you will. He seemed to think you might get lost and so he was keeping an eye out for you. He let me know where you were."

How the hell was she supposed to interpret that statement? "It didn't look like a man," she said, feeling stupid. "It was like some sort of shadow."

Tim grimaced. "Yeah, he does that. I'll introduce you, if it'd make you feel better to see that he is nothing but a man." He sounded hesitant about this, as if he didn't want to. Summer must have given him a look, because he added, "Been a while since you've been on the rez?"

She felt her cheeks heat. "Is it that obvious? I haven't been here since I was twelve and so far I've gotten lost and seen an *associate* of yours." She knew she was not putting forth the most competent of first impressions. Why would anyone trust her to make decisions about a teenager at this point?

The lazy grin lifted up the other corner of Tim's mouth. How old was he? He had that kind of ageless face that meant he could be anywhere from twenty-five to forty-five. Her eyes moved to his hand—well, his wrist, as his hand was still resting on the roof of her car. Now she was just being ridiculous.

And the way he was grinning at her made it pretty clear that he felt the same way. God, she was screwing this up so badly.

Desperately she remembered the reason she was here in the first place. "Where's Georgey?"

Tim shifted, his hips moving side to side and she was absolutely not staring at the fluid motion of his body. Really, really not. He brought his hands down under the door. No ring. Why was she even looking? She wasn't. She was only going to be on this reservation long enough to do… Something with Georgey. To make sure Georgey was well cared for.

"My deputy is keeping an eye on him. Don't worry—the boy isn't going anywhere."

She stared up at Tim in confusion. "You kept him locked up? You promise me you wouldn't!"

Something in his face changed—closed, almost. "I didn't lock him up," he said in a dull voice. "I know you don't know me and I know that you don't know how things work here, but I'm a man of honor."

Her cheeks got even hotter. Why was it so damned hot out here? "I'm sorry—I didn't mean to—"

Tim gave a little shake of his head and stepped back from the car. "You can follow me. I won't let you get lost." Then he turned on his heel and walked back to his cop car. As Summer watched, he opened the car door and set one foot in the vehicle, but then turned and stared off into space behind her. He touched two fingers to his forehead in a small salute and Summer twisted in her seat to see if there was really a man back there. But there was nothing. Nothing but grass and more grass.

Sheriff Tim Means was right about one thing. She didn't know him and she had no idea how things here worked.

www.ingramcontent.com/pod-product-compliance
Lightning Source LLC
Chambersburg PA
CBHW060940120626
46557CB00003B/1081